The Woman at Ox-Yoke

A Western Duo

The Woman at Ox-Yoke

A Western Duo

Lewis B. Patten

Thorndike Press • Chivers Press
Waterville, Maine USA   Bath, England

This Large Print edition is published by Thorndike Press, USA and by Chivers Press, England.

Published in 2001 in the U.S. by arrangement with Golden West Literary Agency.

Published in 2001 in the U.K. by arrangement with Golden West Literary Agency.

U.S. Hardcover 0-7862-2476-2 (Western Series Edition)
U.K. Hardcover 0-7540-4712-1 (Chivers Large Print)
U.K. Softcover 0-7540-4713-X (Camden Large Print)

The text of this Large Print edition is unabridged.
Other aspects of the book may vary from the original edition.

Set in 16 pt. Plantin by Elena Picard.

Printed in the United States on permanent paper.

British Library Cataloguing-in-Publication Data available

Library of Congress Cataloging-in-Publication Data

Patten, Lewis B.
　　The woman at Ox-Yoke : a Western duo / Lewis B. Patten.
　　　　p. cm.
　　Contents: Guns in Greasewood Valley — The woman at Ox-Yoke.
　　ISBN 0-7862-2476-2 (lg. print : hc : alk. paper)
　　　1. Ranch life — Fiction. 2. Colorado — Fiction. 3. Large type books. I. Title.
PS3566.A79 W66 2001
　813'.54—dc21　　　　　　　　　　　　　　00-067301

Table of Contents

Guns in
Greasewood Valley

Chapter One

The two brothers came down Salt Creek of a Saturday morning, their spirits lightening somewhat as they put this distance between themselves and the sprawling ranch, between themselves and the bitter words of a quarrel.

Nine hot, dusty miles stretched between the ranch and the town of Salt Creek. All the way they had passed the familiar scattering of homesteaders' hewed-log shacks, each with its patch of green farmland that force had wrested from the greasewood. Alkali glistened white over the ground, like snow in winter. Here at the lower end of Salt Creek, alkali and greasewood, hardpan adobe soil and poverty seemed to go together.

Tom Roark, younger of the two brothers — he had just turned twenty-two — asked: "What did I do wrong, Day? Why does she light into me like she did this morning?"

Dayton Roark shrugged. His long lips thinned out with a vague bitterness. A guilty conscience could make a woman's tongue sharp. He could have told Tom what all the country knew: that his brother's marrying Roxie had been a mistake; that it was not in Roxie to stay faithful to one man, even her husband; that if she wasn't meeting with Rich Turnbull, she was meeting someone else. Saving himself this unpleasantness, and the fight sure to follow, he said sourly: "She'll be over it by the time you get home. Don't let it bother you."

He was wondering if it would not be kinder to tell Tom himself, rather than let him hear it in a saloon or on the street. It would be, he decided, but still he held off. His habit of easing Tom over the rough places was strong, and he still held to the hope that Roxie might change, or that Tom would not hear. Besides, a man doesn't tell another such a thing about his wife without earning himself a fight. And a fight with Tom, Day knew, would destroy the closeness of the tie between them.

Damn Roxie and her long rides! Damn whatever it was in her that made her different from other women!

Reaching the limits of the town, where green cottonwoods on either side laced their arms across the narrow road and made a cool lane beneath, Day looked at his brother, forced a grin out of his moody sourness, and lifted his sorrel into a run. Instantly Tom was his light-hearted self, the fight with Roxie forgotten. He yelled shrilly as he pounded along beside Day.

Clattering into town, they scattered pedestrians and buckboards like chaff before them and pulled up to a stiff-legged, jolting stop before the saloon on Main Street. Dayton swung a leg over the sorrel, dismounted grinning, and looped his reins about the rail. He nodded at the oldster who lounged, hat cocked against the sun, on the bench beside the batwing doors.

"Hi, Amos! The beer cold this morning?"

Amos Leach, red-bearded and blurry of eye, croaked good-naturedly: "Hell, Day, I ain't had a chance to try it yet."

Tom growled: "Or ain't had the money."

Day laughed. "Come on in, then," he invited. "I'm buying."

Behind Day as he followed the eagerly shuffling Amos, Tom muttered — "Chump." — and Dayton shrugged.

Day would always remember Amos Leach as he had been ten years ago when Day himself had been going to school. Amos had been a top hand and a good man in a fight. Day guessed he'd never see the man, broken and beaten and drunk, without wanting to help him. He quickly sobered, wondering if

11

faithless Roxie would do to Tom Roark what a woman had done to Amos Leach.

There were taller men at the bar than Dayton Roark when he lined up, but he was the one who drew the eye. In his middle twenties, he was built ruggedly, as though planned for hard usage. His features were somber, in repose, but his smile had a warmth that invariably brought an answering smile.

Hard-working was Dayton, carrying most of the load on their big 3R Ranch. His huge hands carried rope burns and calluses. His face showed the buffeting of summer's sun and winter's wind. Blue eyes, startling in so dark a face, and hair worn long for lack of a barber nearer than Grand Junction, completed the picture of Dayton Roark, rancher, except for the usual rider's clothing — boots, tight-legged pants, plaid shirt, and short vest. His hat brim was wide and turned down in front.

Dayton Roark liked these Saturday trips into Salt Creek, liked even the unvarying pattern they took. There were these few beers in the morning, then the buying of supplies to be hauled to the ranch in Doggie Sanders's freight wagons. There was dinner at the restaurant, the warmth and liking in Kate Bradshaw's eyes, and her gently mocking banter. As the long afternoon wore away, he would loll in the shade, talking over carefree days when responsibility was only a word that had no meaning. In the evenings he would have supper at Kate's house, and afterward there would be a dance.

He shifted his foot on the bar rail now, contented and satisfied. He had his problems, but he had his pleasures, too. His hand, reaching out for his beer glass, halted abruptly. His head swiveled toward the end of the bar.

". . . seen 'em sneaking away at daylight when I was coming off the mountain." The words were spoken by a man far gone in liquor, but were plain — too plain.

Even as he moved, Day's mind was racing. This drunk, Vince Brewer, rode for a pool of the homesteaders. Knowing his range, Day felt sure he could be speaking of only one cabin, of only one couple.

Vince's companion, big Sam Yockey, saw Day coming, and his eyes took on the furtive shine of a cat caught in the henhouse. Sam's urgent whisper — "Shut up, Vince!" — only egged the man on.

"Why'n hell should I shut up? I seen 'em plain as day. It was Roxie and Rich, and they'd been there all night!" He cackled meaningfully.

Every sound in the saloon abruptly ceased, and the smack of Day's fist as it crashed into Vince's mouth was as startling as it was unexpected from this man who liked most everyone, and who had such a strong tolerance for their weaknesses.

Tom shoved old Amos Leach aside and moved down the bar. His face was white with rage, his lips working, but Day, watching him, saw the dawning of a sick knowledge in his eyes.

In rage, Tom turned from the prostrate and sodden Vince to Day. "You didn't shut him up quick enough! I heard what he said. Why didn't you let me hit him? Why don't you stay out of my business?" He swung toward the bar. "Vince is a liar!" he shouted. "A damned dirty liar! Anybody want to disagree with that?"

The men at the bar concentrated their attention on their drinks. Their silence seemed only to infuriate Tom. His voice rose. "I'll kill the man that . . . !" He stopped, trembling violently.

Day took hold of his arm. "Come on, Tom. Let's go."

Tom turned his eyes, black and bewildered, on Day and shook his head. But he followed his brother out into the dust and dazzle of the street. His clean-lined, narrow face was ghastly. His voice was a shocked whisper.

"It's true, isn't it, Day? You tried to shut him up so I wouldn't know?"

"This is no place to talk. Get on your horse."

Riding, Tom spoke again, bitterly. "Everybody knew it but me. I guess I did, too, only I wouldn't let myself believe it."

Heading nowhere, simply riding, they rounded the corner past the bank and drew abreast of Salter's Mercantile. Something he saw on the boardwalk brought Tom wheeling around, off his horse before the animal reached the hitch rail. Helpless, but not interfering because he had already interfered too much and too publicly, but acutely aware of Tom's torment, Day followed and swung down behind him.

Rich Turnbull stood on the walk, talking to his father, old Emil Turnbull, and the inevitable cigar rolled back and forth between his heavy lips.

Tom called — "Rich!" — and moved forward.

Rich glanced at him, saw his rage, and for a moment showed uncertainty. Then his glance went to Dayton, became sardonic, mocking, even triumphant.

Tom swung before he had quite reached

15

Rich, and so his fist made an arc through thin air. There was youthful clumsiness in Tom, who was too tall, too thin to be an expert fist fighter. Rich, overly heavy of shoulder, long and lean of torso, plucked the cigar from his teeth, dropped it, and still had time to land a solid blow in Tom's face.

Tom's forward momentum lent this blow force, and it stopped him dead. Squat Emil's eyes glittered, and he swung toward the pair, but Day stopped this.

"Emil!" he snapped curtly. "Stay put! Don't you think Rich is big enough for Tom?"

Tom's nose spurted bright blood, although he seemed entirely unaware of it. Outweighed by a full thirty pounds, only young Roark's fury could carry him through this. Arms windmilling, slowly he drove Rich back toward the edge of the walk. Stepping off unexpectedly, Rich lost his balance and fell, sprawling.

Tom jumped, doubling his legs under him, and both his knees drove squarely into Rich's thick chest. Wind came out of the big man, and sickness came into his face. Tom straddled him, raining blows into his face in abandon, mouthing bitter curses. Rich's head rolled as he tried to escape. His thick lips turned bloody beneath the savage blows.

Sly grins appeared on the faces of the men in the crowd that had quickly gathered. Someone murmured: "He won't be kissing nothing for a while, I reckon." But the grins disappeared swiftly enough as Day swung his head, searching for the speaker. Then Day stooped and gripped Tom's shoulder.

"All right, Tom. You've done enough."

Tom rose dazedly, but obediently. Rich Turnbull sat up, glaring at the two from eyes that were already beginning to swell. He wet his puffed lips with an experimental tongue. Poison began to be distilled in his eyes. He opened his mouth to speak, but Day cut him short sharply.

"You're getting off easy. If I was in Tom's shoes, I'd kill you."

Tom had mounted, and the pound of his horse's hoofs was a diminishing sound as he raced his mount up the street, under the cottonwoods at the turn, and out onto the Salt Creek road that led to the ranch.

Something about this scene stirred recollections in Day, and he had an odd feeling that all this had happened before. For a moment he couldn't remember where. Then he had it. And suddenly Rich Turnbull was again only a foul-mouthed kid, sitting in the dust, bawling and wiping blood from his nose with the back of his hand. A vengeful kid, Rich Turnbull had been, never forgetting an injury until it had been paid off in full, perhaps not even then.

Rich now was snarling: "You'll be sorry for this, damned sorry. We'll . . ."

But old Emil barked sharply, interrupting: "Shut up!" Emil prodded his son to his feet with the toe of a boot, earning a bitter glance for his grumbled comment: "A skinny squirt alongside of you, and the hell of it is he whipped you!"

Somewhere in the melting crowd a man snickered. Rich and Emil marched defiantly toward the saloon, a tall man and a short one, the backs of their necks a dark, angry red.

A voice came out of the street: "Looks to me like wearing guns might be coming back into fashion."

Chapter Two

Dayton Roark finished tying his horse and crossed the walk to enter Salter's Mercantile. The urge to leave town, to follow Tom, was nearly irresistible. No telling what the kid might do when he got home. Roxie would probably egg him on, defying him.

Molly Salter, sixteen and pretty in her bright print dress, stepped aside as Day entered. Only when he saw Molly did the full realization strike Day of how ugly had been this fight and its implications. Suddenly pleasure was gone from the day.

He made his purchases for the ranch from a penciled list, patiently enduring Otto Salter's embarrassment, his too cheerful small talk. Then he headed for the restaurant.

How little it sometimes took to upset the uneasy balance of peace. For five years now he had fought the Turnbulls' greedy acquisitiveness with everything except violence. When the bank, that Emil controlled, tried to foreclose on one or the other of the homesteads on Salt Creek, Day had put up the money to prevent the foreclosure. Even so, the Turnbulls had acquired a full third of these homesteads, perhaps realizing, as did Dayton, that hay was the final measure of how many cattle a ranch would support.

Approaching Kate's restaurant, Day shrugged, but he could not shrug away the oppressed feeling that was like a weight in the back of his head. His greeting to Kate lacked its usual warmth, and he knew from her own grave restraint that she had witnessed the fight.

Straightforwardly she asked him: "Do you remember when we were in the sixth grade and Nash Wilcoxon beat Rich up?"

Day nodded soberly. He had no words, but he and Kate each knew the thoughts of the other. Three nights after that fight of which Kate had spoken, Nash's horse, in the barn behind the house, had been hamstrung and left thrashing and screaming on the floor.

Kate pleaded: "Be careful, Day. Maturity and power haven't improved Rich any."

He tried to put reassurance into his smile, as he touched her hand on the counter. It was cool and smooth. All of Kate was cool and smooth on this hot day, from the top of her shining dark head to her trim ankles.

She made no move to withdraw her hand, but slow color seeped into her face. Her soft gray eyes held an odd expression, one that puzzled him.

He wondered abruptly why Kate had not married, for her effect on him was heady today, dimming the violence of the fight he had just witnessed. Intense awareness of one another was static in the air. Day became aware, suddenly and for the first time, that his thinking of Kate had been limited entirely to these times when he was with her, and it struck him that perhaps he was being unfair to her.

He murmured: "Katie, I think I take you too much for granted."

Her lips curved in a pleasant smile, and her color deepened, but her tone reproved him. "You think too much of work, and of Tom. Do you ever allow yourself the time to think of what *you* want?" She pulled her hand loose with a gesture of exasperation and turned toward the kitchen.

Day watched her go, noticing how softly curved were her hips, how slim her waist, how full her breasts. He felt the heat of embarrassment burning on the back of his neck. He surprised himself, for he did not usually think of Kate as a woman. Kate was honest and straightforward and had even been a bit of a tomboy. Day rolled a cigarette thoughtfully. *You grow up with a girl,* he thought, *pull her pigtails, and shoot marbles with her on the dusty school grounds. You know her so well you do take her for granted.* But now he could remember times when she had seen him unexpectedly, and he could remember the change that had come into her eyes. Maybe Kate's thinking of him had not been limited to the time when she was with him. A vague excitement brushed him. He wished she would come back so he could straighten out his confused feelings.

He heard the steak sizzle as she dropped it into the pan. The door opened behind him, and he swung his head. Lewt Grimes, twisted and malformed, slipped through the door with his habitual unobtrusiveness and grinned shyly at Day.

"Morning, Dayton. Mister Salter said I'd find you here."

"Hello, Lewt. You want me to send those two men down Monday to help put up your hay?"

Lewt Grimes held the homestead that bordered the 3R on the lower end. He was almost an employee of the 3R, since at roundup he rode full time with the regular crew, and worked for the 3R other times when there was need. He possessed that strange gentleness toward animals so common in cripples, as though he realized that only animals accepted him without prejudice because of the unkind fate that had given him a twisted body. "A good man with horses," the old man had called Lewt before he died, and now Day used him whenever he could to break out his colts.

Day sent men each year to help with Lewt's haying, partly as a bonus payment for the hay, partly because he liked Lewt.

Lewt shook his head. "I ain't going to be ready for another week. It's something else, Dayton."

Kate came from the kitchen, carrying a steaming platter of steak and fried potatoes. For an instant Day forgot Lewt, just looking at her. That his frank admiration pleased her showed in the curve of her red lips, in her sparkling eyes, in the hastened rise and fall of her breasts.

She stood before Lewt, her color high, and avoided Day's eyes. "What will yours be, Lewt?" she asked, a sudden gentleness coming into her voice.

"I reckon nothing, ma'am. I just come in to see Dayton."

Day grunted between mouthfuls: "Bring him a cup of coffee, Kate." As Kate moved

23

away, he turned to Lewt. "What were you saying?"

"My cattle's gone, Dayton. Every last head of 'em . . . vanished, gone. I rode all day yesterday and the day before, looking. Turnbull's got riders all over that country, and I asked some of them, but they ain't seen none of mine, either."

Dayton laid the fork down beside his plate. He said quietly: "That ain't possible, Lewt. Cattle couldn't get off that mountain without Turnbull's riders knowing it. If it was rustlers, they'd take Turnbull's white-faces, not your milk-pen stuff. Anybody else missing any?"

"They're all busy putting up hay. I ain't talked to none of 'em. I wanted to see you first."

Day rose.

Kate moved toward the counter and began to gather up his dishes. She asked: "Supper, Day?" Her eyes were anxious.

He tried to grin at her. He said: "I'll have to let you know, Kate. I don't know whether I'll be in town tonight."

Dread was like black thunderheads piling up in his mind. There had been signs all along the way. Trouble never starts without plenty of signs pointing to it beforehand. A man usually ignored those signs, if he didn't want to see them. Dayton guessed he couldn't ignore them any more. Here was something tangible — and dangerous.

Dayton's father, who had settled the 3R on the heels of the Ute evacuation, who had lived in the days of bountiful grass, had not been able to see the value of valley-grown hay. But now the country was changing. With each valley lined with homesteads, with barbed wire fences strung, with the homesteaders' saddle and work stock pasturing in the bottoms all year around, grass for winter pasture was growing scarce.

The Roarks' 3R outfit carried fifteen hundred head. On Roark Ridge, a finger of Salt Creek Plateau pointing southward toward Grand River and reaching nearly to it, there was summer grass in abundance for all these cattle and for the small scattering of homesteaders' young milch stock as well.

Nowadays, the 3R stacked for winter use some five hundred tons of hay from its home place, bought another two or three hundred from nearby homesteads. But it wasn't enough. Day had seen that for several years. Cattle came through the winters weak and thin. A man almost had to figure a ton of hay to the head. It meant buying more. At the last, it would mean crowding out the Turnbulls, or being crowded out by them.

Or it meant encouraging and helping the homesteaders to clear more land, in a search for something more than poverty and slow starvation.

To the Turnbulls, the solution to the problem was different. They could see only extension of their ranch's boundaries as the answer. The disappearance of Lewt's cattle, Day suspected, was a step in this direction. The reaches of Salt Creek Plateau, and the deserts of Utah to westward, could swallow Lewt's twelve head without a trace, could swallow a hundred times twelve. The homesteaders, their small herds gone, would be left tending their small patches of hay that produced only ten or twenty tons each at seven dollars a ton.

They would quit, and the Turnbulls, through the bank, would acquire their land and probably turn it back into winter pasture. Day couldn't raise the money to buy out more than a small handful of the homesteaders.

Anger began to rise in him. Why couldn't a man be content with what he had? If the Turnbulls and the Roarks together would pitch in and help the farmers extend their fields, enlarge their ditches, and guarantee them a fair price for their hay, all trouble could be avoided. But it was too late now to approach the Turnbulls with a proposition like that. There was Tom. And there was such a thing as pride.

Lewt Grimes was waiting patiently, his coffee untouched and turning cold on the counter.

Day smiled at Kate, failing to conceal his worry. "Don't fret about tonight, Kate."

He yanked the door open, let Lewt precede him, and followed onto the boardwalk.

"Don't say anything about this business of your missing cows, Lewt. No use getting folks riled up until we're sure. I'll ride with you, to see what we can find out. But I've got to go home first. I've got to see Tom."

This delay, of course, would reduce his chances of finding tracks, for thunderheads were piling up even now over the back end of the Plateau that was Turnbull's range. He felt he was being unfair to Lewt. But he had to see Tom. He had to try to straighten out this Roxie business. He had to know what Tom meant to do.

Lewt murmured apologetically as they crossed the street: "You're too busy a man to fool with my little bunch, Day. Tell me what you had in mind to do and I'll have a go at it myself."

Day shook his head. "You wait for me. One man can't do much. I could be wrong,

Lewt, but this looks like a squeeze to me. They're squeezing . . . and I guess you know who I mean . . . and they'll squeeze the rest of the homesteaders. You could hang on, maybe, because there's only you to worry about. But how about the men who have got half a dozen kids to feed? No, this is not only the homesteaders' trouble. It's my trouble, too. I've got to have hay, Lewt. More than I'm getting now . . . a lot more if I intend to stay in the ranching business. I'll pick you up at your place tonight. By morning, we can be damned near to Utah. I'm betting that old Emil is too tight just to drive cattle clear over there and leave them. I've got a hunch he'd sell them. It's a lead worth trying, anyway."

Lewt passed before Salter's Mercantile, watching Day untie his horse. Molly Salter came from the store and walked up the street toward her home. Lewt Grimes transferred his attention to Molly, and Day could see the wistfulness in the twisted little man's expression, the candy-store look that was piteous because it had no hope of fulfillment.

Chapter Three

Riding past Molly, Day thought how prettily she walked with her sixteen-year-old consciousness that she was nearly a woman, yet with none of the mature surety of her appeal that was so evident in Roxie. He thought: *Tom should have waited for Molly. She's been crazy about him since she was twelve.*

Gloom settled over him. Here was Molly, eating her heart out over Tom, Lewt eating his out over Molly, and Roxie with everything she ought to want and throwing it all away because to her every man was a challenge that had to be taken up. He crowded his horse, for it occurred to him only now that he might have underestimated Tom's capacity for violence. Suppose Tom killed Roxie? Day's startled horse leaped forward under the involuntary spurs.

How well did he really know Tom? How well did anyone know a person he lived with, even grew up with? Well, whatever Tom had decided to do, it was likely done now. Killing a horse in this heat would neither change nor avert what perhaps had already been done.

But as peaceful Dayton Roark drew his horse into a trot, in him anger was growing, and hate for the greed of the Turnbulls who could leave neither a man's land and cattle nor his wife alone. Dayton Roark, who had fought with peaceful means, was near a turning point.

Out at the 3R ranch house, Roxie Roark watched Tom ride in. Concern brought her out onto the long verandah. She could see the pallor of his face, blotched with red where Rich Turnbull's fists had left their marks. She could mark the tenseness in Tom, an indication that his high temper was at the boiling point.

He dismounted, dropped his horse's reins, and strode toward her, a slender, tall man who was personable and pleasant, but who had no depth. As he drew near, the pallor left his face, and it turned red. He vaulted to the porch, grabbed her arms, gripping until she cried out, and still he said nothing.

"Tom! Stop it! What's the matter with you?" This was the way she normally reacted to his impetuousness, but now beneath her words was the sick knowledge that

Tom had at last heard the vicious talk. Gossip was ugly, and Roxie was aware that it was being particularly cruel toward her. She had known from the glances turned on her in the town of Salt Creek, looks that mirrored everything from leering satisfaction to disdain.

"You slut!"

Tom flung her away from him. She caught her heel and sprawled on the verandah, her dress swirling upward and exposing her shapely legs.

A rider, passing between bunkhouse and blacksmith shop, paused and stared, then moved into the murkiness behind the blacksmith shop door. Ching, the cook, peered through a window and discreetly withdrew.

Roxie shifted and pushed her dress down. Anger began to stir in her. She saw the wavering in Tom, the indecision and characteristic hesitation, but still there was guilt enough in Roxie to force her to control her anger.

Pain twisted Tom's face. The muscles at his temple bunched as his jaws clenched.

Suddenly pity and shame touched Roxie. She asked in a tight, small voice: "Just what are you accusing me of?" But she knew, and the knowledge was bitter.

"Rich Turnbull," he spat at her. "Why?

Why did it have to be him? How could you stand to . . . ?"

His hands went to his face, covering it. When he dropped them and looked at her, such wildness flared in his eyes that, for a moment, Roxie was afraid. Then with a muttered curse, he dropped his hands to his sides, and the violence was gone.

Denial was on Roxie's lips, denial of infidelity, and an explanation, but it was never uttered. Tom took the verandah steps two at a time, leaped on his horse, and galloped hard up the winding gravelly bed of Salt Creek.

She watched him go, her face expressionless, but within her was emptiness, hurt, and utter loneliness. The innate honesty in her understood his condemnation of her even if she could not forgive his refusal to allow her to say a word in her own defense. She knew she had given the people in this country enough to start their tongues wagging. Unaccepted, lonely, she had done a lot of riding by herself. This and only this was what the talk had fed upon until that unfortunate episode at the old sheep camp. That particular morning, two weeks ago, she had risen early, unable to sleep, and had ridden out before even the cook was astir. The chill in the air and the wish to rest had turned her toward the old cabin at sunup, not knowing it was occupied.

Even now, she shuddered at the thought of all she had seen in Rich Turnbull's eyes and voice when she had found him there. She felt like a harlot, remembering his hands upon her. She had fought him off, finally had struck him full in the face with a stick of firewood as thick as her arm. Running, she had left the place, with Rich after her, still convinced that she was only being coy. Someone must have seen them. This had to be what Tom blamed her for. Only Tom had found her guilty of being what Turnbull had tried to make of her.

Roxie had her own kind of strict honesty, and this forced her to admit that it was only the act of infidelity of which she was innocent. In her thoughts she had been unfaithful to Tom. Dissatisfaction and the feeling that life was hurrying by were partly responsible for this. Roxie wanted children, and Tom had given her none.

Shrugging miserably, she went to her room and began to pack a small bag. She called Ching and said: "Have someone hitch up the buckboard. I'm going to town."

There was a train through Salt Creek at nine. She'd catch that.

She slipped hastily out of her clothes and

began to select what she would wear from her generously filled closet.

She emerged from the house, a small, shapely woman dressed in a gray wool suit, chosen because it would not show dust. Her hair, gleaming black, was drawn away from her face and knotted into a bun low on the nape of her neck. She was walking toward the buckboard when Dayton thundered into the yard.

Day's voice was harsh. "He kicked you out." It was a statement, not a question.

Roxie shook her head, with the anger of the unjustly accused in her.

Dayton looked rock-hard, grim, and there was no warmth in him.

Roxie said with asperity: "I don't suppose it would do any good to try to explain. Tom has decided that gossip is to be believed, and so have you." She thought there was softening in Day, but could not be sure. Her shoulders lifted wearily. She said: "I'm leaving. I have done nothing wrong, but I have been dissatisfied, and have not been a good wife." She could feel tears forming behind her eyes, and exerted all her will to force them back. She would not have him think she was begging.

He swung off his horse and came to her. His eyes were troubled and in them were pain and self-blame. He said: "Stay, Roxie. A man is sensitive and proud. Tom has not been blind to your dissatisfaction. The two of you have quarreled a lot. Put that with what he heard today, with his feeling of failure where you are concerned. Give him a chance to think it out."

She shook her head, smiling faintly. "A woman has pride, too, Dayton. No, I'm going."

There was a sag to Day's shoulders, a tired discouragement in his eyes. "Where will you go?"

"To Grand Junction for now. After that . . ." — she smiled — "who knows?"

He helped her to the buckboard seat. He said "We'll miss you, Roxie." — and he meant it.

Roxie's lower lip trembled, and she knew she was going to cry. Not trusting herself to speak, she slapped the team with the reins, and whirled out of the yard. Reaching the road, she turned, saw him still standing there, and raised a small, gloved hand. Day waved, then turned toward the log blacksmith shop.

Roxie kept the buckboard team at a trot, although the day was hot and still. Behind her, to the north and west, thunderheads piled up, towering, immense, their tops white and fluffy, their cores a menacing gray. On all sides rose the great ridges of Salt Creek Plateau, for Salt Creek was only a gash that water had ripped through it in ages past.

The valley lay, broad and twisting, on either side of the creek. Then the land sloped upward, in cedar-clad benches. Where the cedars left off, the brushy slides began, sloping steeply to the rimrock that, perpendicular and ever changing in aspect, rose a sheer distance, varying from three to six hundred feet, and was crowned by the deep green of spruces before the plateau leveled out into its sea of grass.

Driving out of this vast and primitive country, Roxie knew she would miss it, for during her two-year stay here that there had been born in her an abiding love for this land. Depression swept over her, and greater loneliness. Near sundown, with the valley air still, and the sound of cowbells, of shouting men carrying clearly, Roxie came to where a narrow ditch crossed the road, and paused to let her team drink.

A boat came sailing down the ditch out of the tall greasewood, a rudely carved boat with its thin muslin sail spread and bellying in the breeze. The team reared and would have bolted but for Roxie's firm hand on the reins, her gentle: "Whoa now, whoa, boys."

She got down and picked the boat out of the water. A young voice said: "Hey, that's mine!"

He came splashing down the ditch, feet bare and ragged pants rolled to his knees. He carried a broken-handled pitchfork.

Roxie handed him the boat gravely. "I was just admiring it."

She guessed he would be about seven. His hair was brick red, and his thin face was liberally sprinkled with freckles nearly the size of small peas. He took the dripping boat.

"I made it," he said proudly. "I whittled it out of a piece of wood."

Curiosity stirred in her. "What's the pitchfork for?"

"Oh, I'm using that for what I'm doing. I'm throwing weeds and trash out of the ditch for Pa. He don't know I got the boat, but it don't take much time just to let it sail itself down the ditch." He looked at her directly and thoughtfully for a moment. "Who're you?"

"Roxie. What's your name?"

"Roxie Roark?" he said quickly, without answering her question. "You're the one I heard Ma and Pa talking about. They don't like you."

Roxie felt color and warmth flooding her face.

The boy persisted: "Why don't they like you? I do."

Roxie bit her lip. She said: "Let's talk about the boat. How did you know how to make it?"

"I seen a pitcher in a book. I like boats. When I get big, I'm going to be a sailor." He wriggled his bare toes in the dry dust, obviously savoring its warmth after the chill of the water. "Where you going?"

"To town." For a moment Roxie wondered just where she was going, and for a moment she envied this boy's mother and her security. Probably, though, she had half a dozen like him. Probably she was wishing she had fewer to take care of and feed.

A harsh, strident woman's voice shouted from the direction of the creek: "Petee-eee! You git home! Petey!"

The boy started. He said: "I got to get. Ma's hollering fer me."

Roxie smiled. "Good bye," she said.

Petey shook his head in puzzlement. "Can't see why Ma and Pa don't like you. You're purty . . . and you're nice, too."

Roxie murmured: "Thank you, Petey. I like you, too."

Petey, clutching his boat, splashed out of

sight into tall sagebrush and greasewood that bordered the road. Roxie gathered her skirts and climbed to the buckboard seat. She clucked to the team, and the buckboard rolled on down the road, its wheels raising a thin plume of dust behind.

Chapter Four

Petey, torn between the habit of heeding his mother when her voice held this familiar shrillness and his liking for the strange and gentle Roxie, paused as quickly as he was out of sight in the greasewood, then soft-footed it back to a place where he could see the road. He watched her as she gathered her skirts and climbed into the buckboard. He puzzled at the sadness of her expression, but her gentleness, as she had talked with him, lingered and created a warm, pleasant feeling.

"Petee-eee! You get home this minute!"

There was harsh contrast between his mother's shrillness and Roxie's softness. But Roxie's pleasant and lightly perfumed beauty and her quietness had opened a new channel of thought in the boy's mind, and he felt an odd and unreal sureness that his mother had not always been as she was now.

He shuffled across the hay stubble, groping for a pleasant memory that he could make real. Vaguely he recalled stories that had been read to him in a voice not at all like his mother's, quiet songs murmured into his drowsing ears, rustling skirts, and a faint scent of flowers, and his mother's lips warm against his cheek.

Petey could not know how devastating to a woman can be three long years of hardship, hopelessness, and poverty, of mortgages and debts and never enough money for even the bare necessities. He could know nothing about the scars that are left when pride flees before necessity, and a man and woman must ask for credit so they can eat.

He saw her standing before the cabin door now, hands on hips, and guiltily he broke into a trot. At the edge of the field, he took an instant to cache his boat in the high weeds, then he crawled through the fence and approached her.

"Where you been? Who was that up there on the road?"

Petey scratched at the hard-packed ground with a dirty big toe, then looked up excitedly. "Ma, I seen the biggest bear in the country a piece back up the ditch. He come at me a-*whuffing*, but you know what I did? I just jabbed him right in the face with my fork. He let out a yowl, and took out for the top of the mountain. I sure was scared. Took quite a spell before I could get my mind back on them weeds in the ditch." He pretended indifference, but his eyes were carefully watching her face.

She said stonily: "Petey, you know what you get for lying. Who was that up on the road you was talkin' to?"

"Missus Roark. Roxie." He looked steadily at the ground, waiting for the explosion.

Out of a corner of his eye, he saw his father approaching, a bucket of water from the creek in each hand. His father was skinny, stoop-shouldered, and beaten. His blue shirt was patched and thin, and his hat sweat-stained, dusty, and shapeless. There was no enthusiasm in him any more. He simply plodded from one task to the next until night put an end to them all.

Ma's voice raised: "You stay away from that no-'count. Don't you let me catch you talking to *her!*"

"What's wrong with her?"

"Never you mind what's wrong with her! She's no good, that's all. You stay clear away from her!"

Obscure defiance ran through Petey. It made him tremble when she was this way, but he raised his blue eyes, held his chin firm, and said: "I like her. She's purty, and she was nice to me."

All his mother's resentment against the

harshness of living focused itself upon the hapless boy. She snatched him by his thin shoulders and shook him in near frenzy.

"Don't you sass me, you whippersnapper! Don't you sass your ma!"

She threw him across her knees while she belabored his bottom.

Petey, on the verge of tears, not so much because of the pain of the spanking, but more so because of her anger at him, gritted his teeth: *I won't cry! I won't!*

His father's quiet — "That's enough, Ma." — brought an end to the spanking.

Petey scrambled away, facing her, shaking and white-faced, and shouted in a thin, tight voice: "You're mean! That's what you are, pure mean!"

Pa's voice was quiet, but stern. "That's enough, boy!"

"I don't care! I'll talk to her if I want. She's. . . ."

"Petey!"

Petey never ignored this tone in his father's voice. He subsided reluctantly. Ma ran into the cabin, and Petey heard her dry, retching sobs. Pa went into the house, the water buckets forgotten, and Petey heard his low, murmuring voice, and finally his mother's tearless, bitter: "What's happened to me, George? I guess she ain't going to hurt a boy any. I just took out on him all the other things I was frettin' about."

Petey ran for the barn, in deep misery. He guessed there was nothing so awful in all the world as people fighting amongst themselves, especially people that loved each other. Lying in the deep, soft, fragrant hay, he finally sobbed himself to sleep.

At exactly six, Sarah Yockey came through the weed-grown vacant lot behind the restaurant, and entered the kitchen.

Kate Bradshaw untied her apron and hung it up, then smoothed her hair with a gesture that was entirely automatic. "Hello, Sarah. There is roast beef in the oven, and potatoes baking. The roast is about done, and I've let the fire die down."

Sarah was a stringy woman, with an excess of nervous energy, a steady, hard-working woman, who had known nothing better than what she now had and expected nothing better. Big Sam Yockey had given her four big, healthy children and apparently considered his duty discharged, for now he never worked unless it was to obtain the money for his card playing and moderate drinking.

Sam was not overly bright, and neither were his children, a fact well known to Kate.

In winter she taught in the log schoolhouse at the mouth of Salt Creek.

Sarah had an earthy friendliness that made her invaluable to Kate in the restaurant. But gossip, to Sarah, was food and drink. She glanced into the restaurant and whispered: "Did you see the fight this morning?"

Kate nodded, wishing she had left before Sarah had had time to broach the subject.

Sarah whispered: "It was about that woman. Sam was telling me that Vince Brewer seen her and Rich at the old sheep camp at the head of Salt Creek. Vince was shooting off his mouth about it down at the saloon, and Tom heard him and went right out on the street and took to Rich."

Kate said: "I know. I've got to get over to Salter's before they close."

She went out through the restaurant, nodding abstractedly at the two 'punchers at the counter. For months now, she knew, gossip had not been kind to Roxie Roark.

Kate sensed the reason for this. Roxie was different from the local people. She spoke differently; she had a shy restraint, and so had been accused of being stand-offish, believing herself too good to associate with the common herd. Lacking anything concrete, gossip had invented things about her, and

45

there were folks along Salt Creek who were convinced that this affair with Rich Turnbull was one of many, only this time she had been caught.

Kate took gossip with a grain of salt. She knew how viciously unfair it could be. Feeling depressed, she entered Salter's. She looked for Day's solid figure among the crowd and felt a touch of disappointment, when she failed to see him. She wished she knew what had happened to him during the long afternoon.

The store slowly emptied. The sun stained the towering thunderheads to the north and west a flaming copper color, and they threw their glow on the wall of the store, creating an unearthly brilliance, as if the entire world had burst into flame. Slowly, as Kate watched through the window, this brilliance died, and by the time Mr. Salter got around to waiting on her, the clouds had assumed a deep violet color, stained with pink at their upper limits.

The streets of Salt Creek turned drab and ugly with coming dusk, and lamps winked from the windows, one by one. A buckboard drew up before the store, and Roxie Roark climbed down. Coming up the two short steps into the store, she looked at Kate uncertainly.

Kate smiled. "Hello, Roxie. Is Dayton coming back into town tonight?"

Mr. Salter, thin-lipped and chill-eyed with his disapproval of Roxie, moved behind the counter and began to sack Kate's groceries.

Roxie murmured: "I don't think so. I don't know, Kate."

Kate thought Roxie was terribly pale, but put this down to the strain of all that had happened this afternoon, to the quarreling that had undoubtedly ensued when Tom got home. She felt a stir of pity.

Roxie asked: "The train is due here at nine, isn't it? I wonder . . . Kate, would it be asking too much . . . ?" She halted.

Kate moved to her side. She was half a head taller than Tom Roark's wife. "What is it, Roxie?"

Roxie shrugged, smiling apologetically. "I feel so queer. I was going to ask if I could stay at your place until train time."

"Of course, you can," Kate said heartily. She lifted her sack of groceries, said coolly — "Thank you, Mister Salter." — and went with Roxie out the door.

She laid her groceries in the back of the buckboard and started to climb to the seat. Roxie stood rigid and still on the walk, making no move toward the buckboard.

Kate murmured — "Are you ill, Roxie?" — but got no answer.

Suddenly, then, Roxie slumped to the walk. Kate became quickly decisive. To Mr. Salter, watching from the door, she said sharply: "Get that look off your face and lift her into the buckboard! Then get on over to Doctor Slade's house and tell him he's needed at my home!"

By the time Kate reached the small, neat frame house where she and her father lived, Roxie was stirring, murmuring dazedly: "Oh, Kate, I'm sorry. I don't know what's the matter with me." She smiled apologetically. "I'm an awful bother."

Chapter Five

Kate helped Roxie out of the buckboard and up the graveled walk to the door. She lighted a lamp in the parlor, and Roxie sank weakly onto the sofa.

Kate murmured: "Dad isn't home yet. You be quiet, and I'll fix some tea."

Dr. Slade, a round young man, came crunching up the walk in the soft, warm dusk. Kate let him in, then went to the kitchen to kindle a fire in the stove and heat water. When she returned to the parlor with three cups of tea on a tray, she caught the tail end of the young doctor's humorous statement. ". . . and it is a normal thing that happens to women every day. You're going to have a baby, Missus Roark."

For an instant joy, eagerness, and wild elation showed in Roxie's face. "Are you sure? Oh, are you sure?" This faded quickly, to be replaced by hopelessness and despair. Roxie asked: "When? Can you tell me when?"

The medico's face showed that he had heard the gossip, but there was no disap-

proval there. His was the clinical understanding of the passions that drive the
human machine. His voice was soft. "I'd
judge six or seven months. You are about
two or three months along. Don't try to pin
a doctor down on a thing like that, young
lady."

There was a momentary lightening in
Roxie's face. She said calmly: "Thank you,
Doctor."

Assuming a professional joviality, Slade
rose and closed his bag with a snap. "No
overexertion, no long trips by horseback or
buckboard. Eat lightly and get lots of sleep.
See me in a week."

Roxie nodded abstractedly. Slade's steps
crunched down the walk, and Kate heard
him cluck to his horse.

Roxie, staring blankly at the wall, murmured: "This is what I've prayed for. And
it's too late. Tom wouldn't even believe now
that it's his child."

Kate laid a hand on her arm. "Perhaps he
will. But you can't leave here now, Roxie . . .
not the way things are."

"I've got to!" To her voice came a surprised unbelief. "Kate, this just isn't possible! I've done nothing . . . nothing at all,
and yet I'm accused and condemned, even
by my own husband. He wouldn't even give

me a chance to deny it." Her mouth firmed. "But I'll not go crawling back to him." Still, she was not emphatic.

Kate felt her hesitation. "Gossip is vicious and cruel," she said, "and yet the people who repeat it are not always cruel. Don't let this ruin your life and Tom's. Stay here with me for a while and see how things turn out." Kate gave no consideration to the possibility that the gossip would touch her, too.

Tears came to Roxie's eyes, and Kate's own embarrassment at seeing them brought words to her lips. "Trouble is coming, Roxie. I believe even Dayton can see it now."

She told Roxie of Lewt Grimes's cattle and of Dayton's sureness that the Turnbulls were behind their disappearance.

Roxie cried bitterly: "Oh, I've been such a fool! Because Tom was gone a lot, I thought I was neglected. I was bored, Kate, sitting all day long up there with no one but that Chinaman for company. If I'd had the sense to keep busy, to find something besides riding to interest me, this wouldn't have happened. And when Tom did come home, I spent the precious time with him complaining."

The night turned black outside, and after a while Dan Bradshaw came home. He was a small man who had saved enough so that work was unnecessary, but whose mind was ever busy considering people and what caused them to act as they did. Dan Bradshaw knew every soul within fifty miles of Salt Creek, perhaps knew more about them than they knew themselves. He accepted Roxie as naturally as he would any guest, and Kate went into the kitchen to prepare dinner.

Kate in some respects thought as directly as a man. Her sympathy for the homesteaders was boundless, and she was sure that in time the big ranches would eventually give way in the Salt Creek country to those running a hundred head of cattle or less. She had faith in Salt Creek Valley, or Greasewood Valley as it was sometimes facetiously called. She knew that there would be enough land to keep all of the homesteaders in comfortable circumstances, once they had grubbed away the greasewood and planted their land to hay.

She knew that Dayton could have helped more, had he not been forced to strip himself of cash to keep the homesteads from falling into the hands of the bank, and from there into the hands of the Turnbulls. Abruptly Kate examined her own feelings in the matter of the homesteaders, with the idea that perhaps they were more Dayton's thoughts than her own. But she could remember the cold winter days and the unbelievable courage of the homesteaders' children who rode the five, ten, or fifteen miles to school on their plodding, swaybacked ponies, arriving blue with cold but still uncomplaining.

She could remember the raggedness and inadequacy of their clothing, the meagerness of their lunches. She could recall their eyes at the Christmas party as Santa Claus, his beard stained with tobacco and his breath revealing the extent of his own private celebration, had presented each with a paper sack full of candy and fruit.

Her own eyes filled with tears, and anger rose in her. If it wasn't for the Turnbulls, there would be less raggedness for those children, less hunger. And now in their greed, Emil and Rich were taking steps to drive the homesteaders creaking along in their worn-out wagons out of the country for good. The cleared patches would be solid in greasewood in a couple of years, for the Turnbulls did not have the patience for farming and would let the land revert to winter pasture.

The town would die, slowly, of malnutrition. The 3R and the Turnbulls' outfit would become embroiled in a range war that would fill the town with gunmen and riff-raff — and Boot Hill would be more heavily populated than the town itself.

Kate held a teapot in her hand, a delicate thing her father had brought from Denver. But as temper boiled over in her, she hurled it to shatter against the stove. Tears welled into her gray eyes, and she was instantly contrite. She felt an overpowering sense of loss as she swept the pieces into a dustpan. A word behind her brought her guiltily around.

"Temper?" Dan was smiling, gently mocking her. Kate always felt like a small, naughty girl when her father looked at her this way.

She said contritely: "Dad, I'm so sorry. I loved it. But I was thinking. . . ." Anger flared back into her eyes. "I was thinking about the Turnbulls, and about all those homesteaders' children."

Dan had heard the talk around town today. He had drawn his own conclusions. He nodded, sobering. "It makes anybody mad. But don't think about it. Dishes are hard to come by."

He pretended to duck, grinning at her. Tonight she could not make herself go along with his fooling.

She said: "Go sit down. Dinner's ready."

54

Roxie went to bed early, and Dan Bradshaw and his daughter sat in the tiny parlor, pretending to read. Finally Dan looked up.

"You're having as much trouble keeping your attention on that paper as I am. What's the matter, Kate?"

"Oh, it's Roxie and Tom . . . and just everything," Kate said discontentedly.

"Dayton?" her father asked softly.

She nodded. "That's part of it." Her expression turned sweet as she thought of Day, of the way he had talked to her today at the restaurant.

Dan asked: "You making any headway with him?"

"Maybe." She smiled a little. "I thought he showed more interest today than he ever has before. Darn it, Dad, I can't change the way I am even for Day."

He said: "We change whether we want to or not. I have noticed the way men look at you." He hesitated and finally got out: "It is no crime for a woman to appear a little helpless, Kate. You were a tomboy, and I did not try to change you, selfishly perhaps, because I knew I would have less worry about you as you grew up. But Dayton thinks of you even now as the tomboy he romped with in school, not yet as a woman. You will have to make him see you as a woman, Kate."

She frowned. "It isn't honest. I'm what I am."

"There are a good many degrees of honesty. You will make him a good wife. You will make him happy. There are times when the end justifies the means."

She got up abruptly. "I'll have to think about that. I don't know."

He changed the subject, his eyes grave and worried. "We are in for some changes, Kate, as you may already have guessed. There will be trouble, fighting trouble. This thing between Tom and Rich will bring things to a head. Emil could stand to play a waiting game, but Rich cannot, not after he has been whipped in public."

"Dad, how will it end? With the homesteaders beaten and gone, will it be with Day and the Turnbulls fighting it out with guns?"

He shrugged. "There's an old saying that might is right, but that good will triumph in the end. That's not always true, Kate. Day will be hampered by his inability to be ruthless, by his honesty, and by his feeling for people. The Turnbulls will be hampered by nothing . . . nothing at all." He got up, folded his glasses, and tucked them into his vest pocket. "Well, worry never averted disaster. Go to bed, Kate."

She forced a smile. "All right, Dad."

She wandered to the window and stared into the night, westward toward the grandeur of moonlight against towering rimrock, against high-piled thunderheads above it. She murmured: "I wish I knew where Day is. I wish I could be sure he is all right."

Chapter Six

Although Dayton Roark waited until a quarter of ten, Tom had still not returned. He could wait no longer, so Day buckled on his .45, took the .30-30 from the rack over the fireplace, and went out into the heavy, still night. A horse stood before the house, saddled and ready, a roll of blankets and slicker tied behind the saddle. Day walked to the bunkhouse, leading the horse. He stuck his head inside the door and spoke to Cliff Rockman, the foreman, who sat on a bunk smoking a pipe and reading.

"I'm going up on the mountain with Lewt, Cliff. Tom's gone. Keep an eye on things."

"You buy that pitman for the mower?"

Day nodded. "Doggie Sanders will be up with the stuff in the morning."

"So long." The foreman gave him a gold-toothed grin. "We'll still be haying when you get back."

Day closed the door and swung up to the saddle. He let the mount pick its own way to the road, for his eyes were still blind from the glare of the bunkhouse lamp. At the road, Lewt waited, a small, hunched figure atop his hammer-headed, bony black.

Wordless, they took the Salt Creek road. After a mile, Lewt asked: "You bring your slicker? You'll need it."

Day grunted his assent.

Lewt asked: "What are you going to do if you do find the cattle? S'posing he sold 'em? What if he just drove 'em off in a gulch somewheres and shot 'em?"

"He wouldn't shoot 'em. I've an idea he sold 'em, and we can find the buyer. You see anything of Tom this afternoon?"

"Uhn-huh."

The miles dropped slowly behind. At eleven they took the trail up through the cedars onto a brushy slide. The moon was out, and the trail plain. The thunderheads still hung motionless, weird and beautiful in the moon's bluish light. A coyote yipped shrilly and was answered somewhere. A wolf howled triumphantly.

Day said — "There goes another calf." — for he had caught the faint, enraged bellow of a cow.

At one, they came out of the rimrock into the high grass of the plateau and followed the cattle trail along the crest of Roark

Ridge toward Turnbull's range.

Lightning slashed through the ominous clouds, and thunder rolled down Salt Creek, echoing eerily from rim to rim. An icy drop of rain stung Day's face. "Here it comes! Get your slicker on." He untied his slicker from his roll of blankets and slipped into it.

Lightning crackled through the clouds in half a dozen places simultaneously, and the rain came, a solid sheet. The horses lowered their heads and laid back their ears, but plodded on.

Day shouted: "No Turnbull riders out tonight. We'll make it through without being seen, and we'll leave no tracks."

Lewt appeared to hunch lower inside his slicker. A flash of lightning showed Day a stream of water running off his hat brim and down his nose. Lewt's disgruntled reply was all but lost in the roar of the downpour. "We'll find no tracks, either."

"Want to dry out and make some coffee? That old line camp's right down this draw."

He got no answer. Lewt was a shapeless bundle atop the ungainly black. They entered a pocket of aspens, slapped across the soggy carpet of wet leaves, and came out into a clearing. A log cabin sat in the middle of it, and beside the cabin a spring seeped out of the draw. Day swung down stiffly, tied his horse under the overhang of the log roof beams, and pushed open the door. He struck a match, found a candle, and lighted it.

Lewt came into the door, shucking out of his wet slicker. He said: "What the hell's the use, Dayton? A man couldn't track a three-toed bull in this weather." He picked up the water bucket automatically and moved toward the door.

Day was rummaging in the cupboard for coffee, and, when he found it, he turned, opening the stove lid and peering into the stove. He said: "I've seen it pour like hell on top of this mountain and be clear as a whistle once you drop off into the desert. There's only two trails coming off, unless you want to ride twenty miles out of your way. We've come this far, Lewt, so we'd just as well have our look."

Lewt shrugged, and gave Day a twisted, apologetic smile. "Warn't worrying about myself. They're my cattle. But I hate to see you go to all this trouble."

Day snorted good-naturedly, and flashed Lewt a grin. "Get the water."

He kindled the fire with shavings, adding to the blaze until it filled the box of the stove. When Lewt came back with the water, he put a pan of it on the stove and threw in a handful of coffee. Lewt rummaged in the cupboard and found a can of beans, which he opened with his knife.

Day said: "Next time I come through here, I'll pack a load of grub. A man appreciates finding a cabin stocked with a little something to eat."

He wolfed the beans, gulped the scalding coffee, and rolled a welcome smoke. By the time he had finished it, the sky had begun to take on a deep gray color. The tops of the aspens were a barely distinguishable line against it.

Day slipped into his slicker. "Let's travel."

At sunup they came to the western rim of the immense plateau. Here the rain was a mere drizzle, and the view across the desert was spotted with drifting patches of white cloud, with blue on the far horizon. By the time they were out of the rimrock, the ground was dry. Day, who had been watching carefully, halted.

"No use, Lewt. There ain't been nothing but deer over this trail for months. Let's go back and try the other one."

Weariness and discouragement ran through him as he thought: *You are taking Emil Turnbull for a fool. He wouldn't risk anything so foolish as this.* But as he considered, he said aloud: "The Three R's been haying for two weeks and still has a couple of weeks to go. Everybody else on Salt Creek is busy either haying or irrigating. He wouldn't expect any of them to be riding, and wouldn't be afraid of getting caught."

Hope began to stir, and it increased after they had come out of the rimrock and into the warmth of early sunlight. For an hour they followed the rim southward and, at last, dropped off on the second trail, steep and twisting, cut in places of solid rock.

As rocky as this was, here at the top, Day expected no tracks, and so looked for none. But when they reached softer ground where the slide began, he dismounted and studied the trail carefully. There were tracks all right, cattle tracks, dim and nearly a week old. Feeling a stir of excitement, he called: "What did you have, Lewt? These tracks look like two cows, a couple of two-year-old steers or heifers, and some calves maybe six or eight months old."

Lewt chortled. "It's them, Day. I seen tracks of a horse, too, a shod horse."

Hurrying now, they mounted, crowding their horses down the steep and narrow trail.

Day was occupied with the consideration of how a man's character will trap him and trip him up. Old Emil Turnbull and his wife, he was remembering, in spite of their affluence still lived in the old original hewed-log cabin that had been their first home when they had settled in this country. They had money in the bank, a lot of it, it was said, but they had none of the comforts that money could provide.

Instead of beef in winter, they ate venison, for that cost nothing. Even Turnbull's riders suffered from his excessive penury for they were forced to ride the wild horses he brought in from the Utah desert, and, when the horses were sufficiently broken from this riding, the old man shipped them east to Denver and brought in another string of wild ones. In this way, he made his cowboys doubly earn their pay.

In the present matter, it was Emil's penny-pinching closeness that had tripped him up. Another man who wanted to get rid of rustled cows for which he had no real use would have shot Lewt's cattle and pushed their carcasses over the rim where they would probably never have been found. But not Emil. Emil could not stand to see anything wasted and so had driven these cattle here. There was no doubt now in Dayton's mind, but that he would find their buyer before the day was out.

To Dayton Roark, this country was relatively strange, for it was seldom that he ever got over this way. But the tracks of the cattle were plain and easily followed. The sky had cleared entirely, and the day had turned hot, its dryness shrinking his skin and stretching it tight across his face. Tipping his hat to shade his face from the glare, he led out across the desert.

In places the wind had scoured the ground clear of tracks, but by continuing along a logical course he and Lewt had no trouble in picking up the tracks again. In the distance, shimmering in the rising waves of heat, rose fantastic rock formations, colored every hue of the rainbow.

They continued on their way until late afternoon, when finally Day glimpsed a windmill in the distance. It marked a ranch that lay in a bowl-shaped hollow, and in its exact center stood the windmill, turning lazily in the breeze. A stagnant pool of water was fed from the windmill's discharge pipe, and a solitary horse stood in the water, nosing the bright green moss. Except for the horse, there was no sign of life.

Day lost the trail he was following a hundred yards from the windmill, where it became overlaid with other tracks of cattle and horses that had come here to water. He cautioned Lewt as they approached the house: "It would not hurt to be a little careful with this." Presently he loosed his hail: "Hello, the house! Anybody home?"

Carrying a rifle, a man stepped onto the sagging porch, squinting across the sun-washed yard at them. His hair was thinning and in disarray, as though he had just rolled from his bed. A week's growth of graying whiskers covered his slack jaw. His eyes were slightly bulbous and looked not at Day's eyes but at his shirt front. His body was heavy and powerful above the waist, but his long spindly legs seemed too thin to carry his torso.

Day said — "Howdy." — and waited for the customary invitation to get down and rest his saddle. It failed to come. His voice became sharp then as he announced: "We tracked seven head of stolen cattle here. If you bought 'em in good faith, I'll give you what you paid and take 'em off your hands."

The man stared, still not meeting his eyes, his face hostile and unfriendly. The muzzle of his rifle shifted slightly, but still did not point directly at Day.

A bunch of cattle, plodding patiently and wearily, filed into the bowl-shaped depression and headed directly for the water. The man on the porch spoke then, his voice cracked and hoarse from disuse: "You followed a bunch of my own strays. Some way or another they got up on the mountain, and a week ago I brought 'em home." He forced a grin with his thin lips and broken, yellowed teeth that was thoroughly unpleasant — more like a snarl than a smile.

Day shrugged. "We'll water our horses. Maybe we'll circle a bit and have a look."

"You calling me a liar, mister?"

Day looked directly at him, his eyes chill and hard, his jaw tightening with anger. "I'm doing just that."

He stared at the man for a full minute, tension and readiness for trouble building in him. The man on the porch lowered the rifle muzzle slowly and carefully until it pointed at the ground. He muttered surlily: "Don't ride in here again, mister. Don't ride in here again making fight talk at Leo Trott. You'll get a rifle bullet in you before you can reach the house!" He turned and started for the door.

Day said sharply: "Lean that rifle against the wall before you go in."

Trott turned baleful eyes on Day, but he set the rifle down obediently. He slammed the door behind him.

Day whirled his horse and rode out of the yard, saying: "We'll find the cattle, and then we'll come back."

Chapter Seven

It was odd, what they saw happening. At this time of afternoon, and likely in early morning, cattle came from all points of the compass, along their plain and beaten trails, to water. Such a thing as this could be seen only in desert country where water holes were scarce and far apart. The animals formed long lines, like the spokes of a wagon wheel, and at their center was the windmill, and the stagnant pool of water.

Patient and plodding were these stringy desert cattle, walking sometimes as much as five miles daily for their drink of tepid, alkali water. Afterward, they would take the same trails, and dark would find them still on their way to grass and scrubby brush.

Day said: "Your cattle are not used to this country. They wouldn't stray far from the water."

Lewt nodded.

Circling, crossing the cattle trails, Day and Lewt gradually increased the diameter of their circle.

The sun dropped low and its rays, slanting through dust, stained the landscape a deep orange. Day realized he was crowding his tired horse too hard, and strove to control his impatience. He said irritably: "Damn it, we're going to have to camp and look some more tomorrow."

Lewt murmured, trying hard to conceal his disappointment: "Hell, let's give it up. I'll come back in a week or so."

Day grunted: "Damn it, I didn't mean that. Get it through your head that there's something in this for me, too." His eyes turned hard. "I could go back and beat it out of that hardcase back there."

"Don't. He's dangerous as a rattlesnake. He's. . . ." Then suddenly Lewt shouted: "There! There they are!"

Out of a draw the cattle filed, following the whitefaces. Two cows led the way, then came a couple of calves, then another bunch of whitefaces. As two steers and another calf appeared, Day sighed with relief.

"All there. They haven't been here long enough to split up."

With a whoop, he touched spurs to his horse and raced toward them. Lewt, grinning from ear to ear and looking like a child atop his huge, bony horse, galloped beside him.

They drove the bunch in to water, but now Lewt was plainly apprehensive. Day tossed Lewt his rifle, saying: "Belly down behind the windmill with this. It'll discourage him if he can't get both of us at once."

"But Day. . . ."

"Do it. He won't shoot me so long as he knows you're out there waiting." He kicked his horse around and rode openly toward the drab, weather-stained shack. The sun was down now, and the cloudless sky was turning rapidly gray. Light faded in the windswept yard.

Day yelled: "Trott! Come out!"

It gave a fellow a queer feeling, standing before a darkened house, calling out a man this way. He noticed that the rifle was gone from against the front wall of the house.

He called again: "Trott! I know you bought the cattle. I'm going to take them. You want your money?"

This brought Leo Trott onto the porch. He said angrily: "I paid a hundred and a half."

"Who sold 'em to you?"

"To hell with you!" Day touched a spur to his horse's flank, gently, and the horse took half a dozen steps before Leo Trott called: "All right."

Day went back. Dusk blurred the man's face until it was only a white patch against the wall of the house.

Trott said: "He didn't give his name. 'Twouldn't have been no good if he had. He was a short feller. Broad. Looked like a toad."

Day grunted: "Emil." He dismounted. "Strike a match. I'll count you out your hundred and fifty."

A match flared, and Day peeled off seven twenties and a ten from his small, string-tied roll. Stuffing the rest back into his pocket, he looked at the surly Trott.

"I'm not making a practice of buying back stolen cattle. Don't forget it."

He handed over the wad of bills. Trott took them with his left hand while his right still held the rifle.

Trott was wordless as Day mounted and rode off toward the windmill towering against the light gray sky. He knew he was silhouetted plainly against it. A spot between his shoulder blades became suddenly sensitive, but he would not turn.

He saw the hunched shape of Lewt as the little man rose from his place beside the windmill. He saw the rifle Lewt carried come to his shoulder, and suddenly Day knew that Trott meant to kill him.

Now all the playing he had done in the Salt Creek school yard came back to him. He threw himself to one side, not leaving the horse, but putting his whole body on one side, his arms going around the animal's neck. Unaccustomed to this, the horse shied.

Trott's rifle roared, then roared again. The .30-30 beside the windmill barked its answer. Day, hanging to one side of his horse like an Indian, but still controlling him, snatched his .45 from the holster and fired under the horse's neck. The horse reared, forcing Day back into the saddle. Again the rifle cracked. Suddenly Day quit the horse altogether and stood spraddle-legged facing the shack. He could see the dim figure of Trott now, and, as the man shifted the rifle barrel to cover him, Day put his sights on the killer and loosed his shot.

The gun bucked against his palm and bright orange blossomed from its muzzle. Trott yelled and dropped his rifle. Day rasped: "Stay where you're at, you damned dry-gulcher, or I'll give it to you dead center!"

Lewt came up, running. He panted: "You was between me an' him, Day."

Trott whined: "Damn you, you busted my shoulder!"

Day said: "Get the horses, Lewt. We're pulling out."

"Ain't you going to help a man? Ain't you going to look at this shoulder?"

Day stared at him steadily, while Lewt caught his gray and brought it to him. Then the little man walked to the water hole and brought back his own mount.

Day swung up, still not speaking.

Trott said weakly: "It ain't human, leaving me like this."

Capitulation was in Day, but Lewt said coldly: "Think about that shoulder next time you're fixing to shoot a man in the back!"

He turned his horse, and Day followed. They cut the small bunch of cattle out at the water hole and started them back toward home, not stopping until they had a full five miles between themselves and Leo Trott's unhealthy presence.

Emil Turnbull's range lay across the back of Roark range, stretching from rim to rim, so that a man traveling from the main plateau onto the ridge had to cross it whether he wanted to or not. In late afternoon, Dayton Roark and Lewt Grimes, unshaven, dirty and incredibly weary, drove the recovered bunch of cattle across this wide domain.

Day had told Lewt earlier: "We'll put your cattle on the point of Roark Ridge. I've got a pair of riders camped up there all the time. They can keep an eye on 'em along with my stuff."

Coming now through heavy, screening serviceberry and oak brush, a rider ahead caused the cattle to stop suddenly. Day whistled and slapped his chaps with his quirt.

The cattle moved on hesitantly, and presently the rider came out of the brush beside Dayton. Day, alert and watching, felt his tight muscles go slack, and he said: "Hello, Vince."

Vince Brewer's narrow face was sullen, and it was plain that he had not forgotten Day's blow and was still resentful. He said: "You look like you'd come a long ways. Strays?"

Day would have answered evasively, preferring to keep Emil's rustling to himself for the moment, but Lewt, who paid a part of Vince's wages, answered: "You might say they'd strayed . . . with Emil riding right behind 'em. Where were you when he gathered 'em up?"

"Hell, Lewt, a man can't be everywhere. You and the rest of the nesters pay me thirty a month, but a man has to go to town once in a while for supplies."

Lewt snorted: "Supplies that come in a brown bottle?"

Day shrugged and nudged his horse down the trail. The cattle had spread out, but as he neared them, they gave up their grazing and moved patiently ahead of him.

Vince, following Day, asked: "What you fixing to do about Emil?"

"There's a sheriff in Glenwood Springs, and a law against rustling."

"You got the goods on Emil?" There was surprise in Vince as he asked his question, and Dayton got the impression that he was being pumped. But the elation in Lewt at recovering the cattle and his weariness brought his words tumbling out.

"You think I'd say a man had rustled cattle if I wasn't sure? Hell, yes, we got the goods on Emil . . . enough to put him in the pen for a couple of years."

They left the range that was Turnbull country, and came down a long slope onto Roark Ridge. On either side, distantly, they could see the rim, could see the blue-razed void where the land fell away into the half-mile deep cañon that was Salt Creek on one side, Dry Creek on the other. Vince Brewer left them here, angling back toward the rim on the Salt Creek side to his camp.

At sundown, Dayton and Lewt left the cattle near the point of the ridge and dropped off onto the trail that led steeply down into the valley.

Lewt Grimes asked: "Did you mean that about going to the sheriff? You think you can make a rustling charge stick against a man as big as Emil?"

"There's only two ways to handle rustlers. Let the law do it, or do it yourself, but there's one thing sure. If we do nothing at all, how long do you think Emil will wait before he grabs off somebody else's bunch? Emil neither needs nor wants the money he gets out of stolen cattle. He wants the homesteaders' cattle stolen because he knows that's the one thing that will make them quit."

Day was not so sure now that he was nearly home. Lewt's doubt regarding the willingness of the law to come in and press charges of cattle rustling against a man with Emil's money and influence was beginning to make itself felt in him. Yet there appeared to be no alternative short of direct action that he knew would touch off open war in the Salt Creek Valley. A man, or ten men, could not patrol enough country to keep this rustling from being repeated. Emil, caught at rustling Lewt's cattle, would probably be less foolish in the future. From here on, it would simply be a carcass here and a carcass there, bullet-riddled, and no proof to show who had done the shooting.

Depression dogged Day as he rode down the lane toward home, as he waved at the hunched shape of Lewt heading downcreek toward his own small shack.

Tom sat, brooding and sodden with liquor, in the hide-covered easy chair in the long front room, a half-emptied bottle beside him.

Day nodded at him, lifting the bottle and taking a long, fiery drink. Tom raised eyes that were bitter and full of pain.

"Where'd she go?" His voice was thick and slurred with liquor.

"Grand Junction. When did you get home?"

"About midnight last night."

"How's the haying going?"

"Haven't been out to look."

Dayton, heavy-lidded with weariness, stared at him and wished he could think more clearly. He said quietly: "Gossip is cruel, and not always true. I'm not sure Roxie had done what we have accused her of doing."

Tom came out of his chair, trembling. "Vince saw her come out of that cabin at sunup with Rich!"

"That's all Vince saw."

"Don't be a damned fool, Day! Don't try to see good in her when there is only rottenness."

"Did you give her a chance to explain?"

"What the hell was there to explain? She's made a fool of me in front of the whole country. She's made it so I want to smash the mouth of every man I see because I know what he's thinking, because I know he's laughing at me!"

Chapter Eight

Shrugging, Day started to turn from Tom. He paused, seeing the sudden desolation in his brother's narrow face. He said: "You are still in love with Roxie. If it wasn't for your pride, even believing she is guilty, you'd take her back."

Anger flared in Tom's eyes, and a denial was on his lips. But the anger died, and the denial was never uttered. He nodded miserably. "I guess I would. But a man has to live with himself, and he has to live with his neighbors. I won't go after her, Day."

"Not even if you were to find out you were wrong?"

Tom laughed, his laugh an ugly thing. "I won't."

Day wanted to ask what Tom would do the next time he met Rich Turnbull, but he forced himself to hold this in, thinking: *Don't plant ideas in his head.* He picked up the bottle, corking it and tucking it under his arm. "This isn't helping any."

Tom glared, and his hands gripped the arms of his chair.

Day set the bottle back. "I'm sorry, kid. I know it's tough. If the bottle helps any, go to it."

He went up the stairs to his room. Exhausted, he turned in, knowing he would be asleep as soon as he touched the bed.

Tom Roark had watched his brother plod heavily upstairs. Curiosity touched him briefly, and he wondered where Day had been. He heard Day's boots hit the floor, heard the squeak of the bedsprings as Day threw his weight on the bed. Silence filled the house, silence that intensified the hammering of Tom's thoughts. He reached for the bottle, uncorked it, and touched it to his lips.

Abruptly and violently, then, he flung it across the room to shatter against the wall. He stood up, trembling, and went toward the door. With his hand on the knob, he hesitated, finally turned, and went to the rolltop desk that sat against the far wall. Out of one of the drawers he took his holstered gun and belt, and an extra box of cartridges that he emptied into his pocket.

Outside, coming night was a thick curtain of velvet spreading across the land, its pale lining still visible in the west. Light shone dimly from the bunkhouse windows. The warm air carried the pleasant, drying smell of cut hay, of steamy corral, of sun-baked sagebrush. The creek's low murmur came to his ears as it tumbled its tireless way toward Grand River. Up in the cedar benches a coyote pack yammered in sharp-toned quarreling. Downcreek, a dog barked, stirred by mysterious kinship and torn between that and loyalty to his two-legged master.

Tom got a horse from the corral, saddled quietly, and rode out the lane to the road. A strange new tension drew his muscles and nerves tight. He rode on, finally turning into the narrow, twisting road that followed the clear trickle that was Dry Creek to the Turnbull ranch.

Twice he left the road to avoid riders, heading toward town. His hand kept straying to the pistol grip at his side as though for reassurance.

At nine, he slipped softly into the Turnbull yard, picking his way carefully around the untidy litter of worn-out machinery, piles of tin cans and trash, until he came to the house.

Lamplight shone from the windows. Water, recently thrown from the door, made a soft shine against the ground. At the back of the one-room, hewed-log cabin was a slope-roofed afterthought that Tom knew was Rich's bedroom. Across the yard, nestling against the huge barn, stood another log building, its roof nearly flat and covered with sod. The bunkhouse.

From the open door of this building came the low talk of the crew and an occasional ribald shout.

Fully sobered by his ride, there was chill in Tom's body now and a clammy sweatiness to his hands. His stomach twitched and jumped and felt strangely empty. His eyes, invisible in the darkness, were wide with wildness.

He opened his mouth to shout, but emitted only a croak. He thought of Roxie and pictured her in Rich's hairy arms. This brought the flame of rage to his brain. The words — *Rich! Come out!* — formed in his head, but still he hesitated, bothered by a new thought picture, that of Rich, lying on the ground, his eyes dull and sightless in death.

All of Tom's life he had avoided killing of any kind. Butchering time on the ranch always found him with an important task elsewhere. He could recall once, when Dayton had shot a horse whose leg was broken, how physically sick he had been, how sickness of spirit had dogged him for days.

Never had he hunted after his first try when he had been twelve, for he could never forget the sudden reduction of glorious antlered action into a mound of dead and shapeless flesh. Knowing now how surely it was not in him to pull the trigger against Rich Turnbull, or against any man, he returned to his horse and, filled with self-hatred, rode back toward home.

He accused himself bitterly of cowardice. It did not occur to him that not once had he thought about the possibility of harm befalling himself in an encounter with Rich. But now his hatred of Rich Turnbull had doubled, for not only had Rich stolen his wife, but also he had shown him his own weakness.

Tonight Tom welcomed the oblivion of sleep. But even as he slept, he had a full realization that tomorrow, and a thousand tomorrows, he would have to live with himself, to face himself, and despair laid a heavy weight against his brain.

At four in the morning, Dayton left the ranch, picking up Lewt a few minutes later, then continuing at a steady pace toward Salt Creek. At seven, he and Lewt boarded the train for Glenwood Springs. All through the

long morning the train puffed upward toward the bare, sere slopes of the Divide.

Just after noon it whistled its way into
the county seat. Dayton and Lewt
alighted and headed immediately for the
sheriff's office. Day, walking fast, said:
"We've got only a hour if we're going to
get back tonight. There's a westbound
train at one-thirty, and no more until that
time tomorrow."

The sheriff was not in his office, but they
found him at a saloon on Main Street near
the river. He was a short, round-bellied man
with a drooping mustache that was stained
from tobacco. His hat, wide-brimmed, was
pushed back to reveal thinning, reddish
hair.

Day hauled up beside him at the bar, grinning faintly, and said: "Hello, Mike."

"Well, I'll be damned! Dayton Roark! I
didn't know you ever took time enough off
from them cows to come to the city."

Dayton's smile was warm, for he liked
Mike Pruitt. He said: "I haven't much time,
Mike. I want to file a rustling complaint."

Mike sobered. "Against who?"

"Emil Turnbull."

"That ain't a very good joke, Day."

"It's not a joke at all, Mike. Emil drove
seven head of Lewt Grimes's cattle over to

Utah and sold 'em to a man named Leo Trott."

Mike Pruitt swiveled his head to put his sharp eyes on Lewt. "Why ain't Lewt filing this complaint?"

"You know damned well why he isn't." Day's smile faded, and his eyes became cold. "You'd tell him not to be a damn' fool. You'd tell him you weren't going to get involved in a nester-cattleman squabble."

"That's what I'm going to tell you, too, Dayton. What you trying to stir up down there? You know damned good and well what'd happen if I arrested Emil. How many head did he take?"

"Seven."

"You get 'em back?"

Day nodded.

"Then what the hell are you squawking about?"

Day stood away from the sheriff, his face cold and intent. "I figure I need the nesters, Mike, because I need the hay they raise. Emil and Rich figure they need the grass the nesters have got fenced in, and they're using this way to drive 'em out. All the nesters have a few head of cattle, milk pen stuff, and, if they lost those cattle, they'd all pack up and leave. Emil and Rich mean to see that they do lose their cattle. And Mike, I

85

mean to see that they don't."

Worry drew furrows in Mike Pruitt's brow. "Don't stir up something you can't handle, Dayton."

"I'll handle whatever I start."

Lewt, who had stood silently beside Day, touched his arm. Anger smoldered in his deep-set, dark eyes. He murmured: "We wasted a trip, Dayton. There's law for the big man in this county, none for the little man."

Color rushed into Mike Pruitt's brown face. His eyes glittered. He growled: "Now wait a minute, you little. . . ."

"Mike!"

Pruitt halted. Finally he managed a thin-lipped smile. He said: "Tell you what, Dayton. I'll come down in a day or two and talk to Emil. How'll that be?"

"No good at all, Mike. I'm not going down in this shuffle, and, if Emil drives the nesters out, I'm done. You can stay here with your heels on the desk for a while. But I'll bring you out of it, or the Turnbulls will."

He turned and went out, Lewt following as unobtrusively as a spaniel. Outside, Day said bitterly: "He'll come down to Salt Creek, all right. He'll tip our hand to Emil and let Emil know he doesn't intend to do a damn' thing about this."

"Then what?"

"Maybe nothing. But if Emil ever gets the idea the law means to let him alone, do you think he'll piddle around with half measures? Hell, no! It's only fear of the consequences that's kept him moving slow so far. If he thinks he's safe, he'll step in and make the fur fly."

Lewt's jaw was set, his eyes fixed straight ahead of him. He asked: "You ever think what a cripple has to put up with?"

Day started, so unexpected was this question.

Lewt went on: "You move into a new country, and people stare at you and avoid you and treat you like you was some kind of strange animal. The kids holler and make fun, even throw rocks. If you stick it out long enough, they get tired of it, and maybe after a while they even begin to think of you as human." There was an odd strain in Lewt's voice, and the blur of moisture in his eyes. "I've gone that far in Salt Creek. It's even got so a few like me." He looked at Day, and his voice was hoarse. "Do you think I'm going to let a two-bit crook like Emil run me out, to go through it all again somewhere else?" He shook his head, and whispered: "He'll have to kill me first."

There was no doubting the desperation in Lewt Grimes. Again, as it had so many times this week, anger rose in Dayton Roark. He had tried the peaceful way. Now he would try the other.

Chapter Nine

Vince Brewer threw one backward glance at Dayton and Lewt as he rode off toward his camp near the rim. As they passed from his sight over a small knoll, he rammed spurs into his horse's ribs, and the animal jumped ahead, galloping through the low sagebrush and high grass.

This trail led southwestward toward the rim on the Salt Creek side. After ten minutes, Vince reached his camp, a graying tent pitched on a small level space beside a spring. A carelessly erected pole corral nearby held a single horse. Vince quickly changed saddle and bridle from the horse he was riding to the one in the corral and, mounting, took a trail that followed the rim back toward the Turnbull range.

Vince was a man of medium height with a sharp-featured face, a sallow complexion the sun could not seem to darken, and a nose that would not have surprised you had it begun to twitch. His eyes were a chilled blue, unsmiling eyes that stored this man's resentment against the good fortune of others and cherished the memory of each small slight to his pride.

Dayton's blow in the saloon had been such. Vince Brewer had considered himself justified in spreading the juicy bit of gossip about Roxie and Rich, and Dayton's fist-in-the-mouth technique of shutting him up was a thing for which he had sworn he would be revenged. He didn't like Dayton, anyway — or Tom, or Roxie. He liked the Turnbulls no better. The lot of them, Roarks and Turnbulls, fell into a class Vince hated, a class of people who, through work and ability and good fortune, had amassed a quantity of worldly goods. Now he was prepared to turn traitor to the homesteaders who hired him and paid his wages, in order to carry this bit of information to the Turnbulls, all for the sole purpose of getting even with Dayton Roark.

After a couple of miles he struck another trail that angled across the back of Roark Ridge. After a half hour's riding, this took him to the drop-off of the trail that led into Dry Creek. Far below he could see the untidy cluster of buildings that marked the Turnbull ranch.

He took this trail, one too hastily and carelessly constructed, and at dusk rode into the Turnbull yard.

Rich Turnbull saw him ride in. Rich had just finished shoeing a horse, and his temper was ragged and short. He had not the patience to cope with the vagaries of animals. Turning from the horse to face Vince, he could not resist a vicious blow with the hoof nippers against the animal's rump. The sharp edge of the nippers raked a long and bloody furrow across the smooth hide, and the horse lunged away, snorting.

Rich scowled: "What the hell do you want?"

Vince swung down off his horse. He stared at Rich for a moment, resentment all too plain in him. Then he turned and remounted.

Rich asked irritably: "What the hell's the matter with you?"

"I was going to tell you something I figured you'd want to know. Reckon you don't care about hearing it."

He reined his horse around. Rich smoothed the irritation from his voice and said: "Sorry, Vince. That damned horse I shod has got me edgy."

Speaking across his horse's rump, Vince intoned: "It's about Emil. Seems he drove a bunch of Lewt Grimes's cattle over to Utah and sold 'em. Dayton and Lewt got the cattle back, and they're going to tell the sheriff."

A scared shine came into Rich's close-set eyes, and he started to bluster. He halted this and turned, bellowing at the house: "Emil! Hey, Emil!"

Emil came through the door, broad and squat and ugly. Seeing Vince, his steps hurried almost imperceptibly. Rich glanced up at Vince and caught the man's gloating grin. Vince was looking at the eye Tom Roark had blackened, at the lips, thickened and blue with bruises. Of these two who could hold grudges, Rich could hold them the longer, could find more satisfying ways of settling them. In Rich's mind he marked Vince as one who would pay, eventually.

Vince said — "You got something to settle with the Roarks, too, looks like." — and laughed uneasily.

Emil came close then, asking: "What's the matter?"

It was Rich who spoke and not at all like a son speaks to his father. "You damned simple old fool! Why didn't you shoot those cattle like I told you to? Now Day's got them back and is going to the sheriff with his story."

Emil's eyes darted back and forth between the faces of Vince and Rich. "How the hell'd he find 'em?" He fixed his suspicious glance on Vince.

Vince's uneasiness plainly increased. "I didn't have nothing to do with it! He tracked 'em! He must've tracked 'em!"

"Through all that rain?"

Rich laughed, his tone conciliatory. "No use worrying about how he found 'em. He did, and that's the important thing. How about Leo Trott? Will he blab?"

Emil shook his head, but there was no conviction in him.

Rich said softly: "Thanks, Vince. Thanks for coming by."

"Thanks? Is that all it's worth to you?"

Rich fished in his pocket, brought forth a worn golden eagle. He tossed it contemptuously at Vince, who caught it. Silence fell between them, a silence that Vince stood for only a moment. Then he muttered: "I got to go. I got to get back."

Rich looked at him steadily without speaking. The speculation in the big man's eyes seemed to put Vince's nervousness on the increase. Abruptly and almost as though he were frightened, he whirled his horse and dug in his spurs.

Rich waited until he was out of sight in the near dark. Then he mounted the saddled and newly shod horse and followed. Ten minutes later a single rifle shot echoed back and forth from rim to rim, diminishing gradually and fading into nothing.

Rich dismounted where he found Vince Brewer's body and walked cautiously to it, nudging it with the toe of his boot. Satisfied that Vince was dead, he walked uptrail and caught Vince's horse, leading it back to where he could load Vince's body.

He surprised himself with the realization that he felt no more emotion over killing Vince than he would have felt over killing a deer, yet this was the first human life he had taken. Feeling no emotion and no regret, there was no need for him to justify the killing to himself. There was only the need to conceal the fact that he had killed Vince, so that he would not have to pay the penalty when the murder was discovered.

Grunting, he hoisted Vince's body up, belly down and head and feet dangling. Vince's horse, not liking this, fidgeted and snorted, rolling his eyes backward at the inert burden. Rich tied Vince down, exerting care that the rope was padded by clothing and never made contact with Vince's bare skin. As an afterthought he removed the gold coin from Vince's pocket. This done, he mounted and headed uptrail, leading Vince's mount.

Already Rich's active mind had planned a way of disposing of Vince, and now his thoughts went ahead, probing every possibility that someone had known Vince had been at the Turnbull ranch.

There was certainty that neither Day nor Lewt had known. Rich felt equally certain that no homesteader had known. Finally he smiled, fished a cigar from his pocket, and lighted it with satisfaction. He was in the clear.

While he felt no remorse at having murdered, he would not have done it had he had not felt it necessary, for it added unnecessary risk to his plans. But Vince, a congenital turncoat, would have betrayed Rich and Emil as quickly as he had betrayed Lewt, for whom in part he worked. Also, because of Emil's greed, another killing lay ahead of Rich, and another risk added to the game that need not have been added.

Rich knew this trail like he knew the back of his hand. He toiled slowly upward, and finally, at a place where it was carved out of solid rock and not more than a foot wide, he dismounted and led his horse across the narrow spot.

Cautiously he inched his way back, past his own horse, past the head of Vince's mount. He untied the ropes that held Vince in the saddle. Working in almost total darkness, there was difficulty in this, but at last it was done.

Again he inched himself upward on the trail until he stood between Vince's horse and his own. Feeling a touch of nervousness, he fished in his pocket, found his jackknife, and opened it. This he jabbed hard in to the chest of Vince's horse, immediately afterward ramming a hard fist directly into the animal's nose.

The horse screamed, a tortured wail that fell across the black void below him. He reared. Rich leaped toward him, yelling and waving his arms, the striking fore hoofs only inches from his head. The horse, off balance, shuffled backward on his two hind hoofs. Again Rich yelled. The body of Vince slid out of the saddle and dropped the sheer hundred feet to the beginning of the slide.

Once again Rich yelled. Behind him he could hear the nervous shuffling of his own horse, could hear the rocks that had been dislodged crashing below. Vince's horse, utterly terrified, gave one last shrill snort, came down on his four hoofs and tried to turn in the narrow trail. A fore hoof went off, came back, and then a hind hoof went over. With his head over the precipice and his rump thrown hard against the rock wall, his shoulder was presented to Rich, twisted and straining.

Rich jumped forward and again jabbed the knife home. With one last surge of power, the horse brought his head around but, in so doing, put both front hoofs over the edge. With an unearthly scream, he went down, and an instant later Rich heard the crash of the animal's body far below. For a full two minutes afterward he heard the rumble of the avalanche he had started.

With unsteadiness in his legs, Rich eased back uptrail until he was past the head of his own horse. He talked to his horse, soothing him, something he rarely did. At a switchback in the trail, he mounted and continued upward, but he was halfway to Utah before he could put the tortured wail of Vince's horse out of his mind.

Rich Turnbull, harder on horseflesh than was Dayton Roark, reached Leo Trott's bleak spread in the late morning. The sun, directly overhead, laid its scalding heat against the ground, and from there the heat rose in shimmering waves that distorted everything in sight. Rich sat tall and ponderous in the saddle, a heavy man who had learned to ride bareback and who now stuck in his saddle like a burr, never using the stirrups at all except as a place to put his feet.

Head down, his horse trudged into Leo Trott's yard.

Rich lifted his heavy voice, and its arrogance brought Trott through the door, a revolver in one hand, the other in a dirty sling across his greasy shirt front. Rich appraised the man, saw the unsteadiness of his eyes, the surly weakness about his mouth and chin. If there had been doubt in him before, there was none now. Trott, like Vince, was a man of shifting loyalties, each shift determined by his own personal advantage. The old Navy pistol, held loosely in Trott's hand, however, forced a change in Rich's direct plan. He had intended riding in, shooting Trott down without so much as a word of explanation.

This suspiciousness in Trott made necessary a certain amount of palavering — enough at least to throw the man off guard. He gave the man a loose-lipped grin. "Always meet strangers with a gun in your hand?"

"You ain't no stranger. You look just like your old man, 'cept you're taller. Get the hell away from here and don't come back."

Rich laughed placatingly. "Wait a minute. Hold on. I want to talk to you."

"Wait, nothing! I said get! I bought some scrubby damn' cattle from your old man and what did it get me? A smashed shoulder. I ain't going to talk to you no more. Turn your horse and start riding before I let daylight through your rotten carcass!"

Sudden wild rage rose to Rich's throat, giving him a choking sensation. His face purpled with the rush of blood upward to it. But there was no arguing with the implacable coldness in Trott's eyes. He reined his horse around, let it take half a dozen steps, then came out of the saddle in a bound, turning, landing spraddle-legged and facing Trott. Trott's gun rose slowly, and the man's slit eyes widened with surprise.

Smoothly Rich's hand went for his gun. Smooth and fast. He was no Earp, no Tilghman, but he had a natural muscular co-ordination that wasted no motion and did no fumbling. His gun was level, its hammer back, while Trott was still raising his own, while the spindle-legged man still drew back on the hammer awkwardly with his left thumb. Carefully noting this small margin of time, Rich did not hurry, sighting meticulously before he let the hammer fall.

Trott, snarling and surprised at first, now turned panicky with the fear that crowded over him. He yelled: "No! Don't do it!"

Rich tightened his finger on the trigger

and loosed his shot. The sound hung flat and without body upon the face of the desert for an instant. Smoke curled from the muzzle of Rich's gun. An unseen force flung Leo Trott backward, and his mouth gaped open to reveal uneven rows of yellowed teeth. He crumpled slowly into the sun-baked yard. Rich left him there, a red stain spreading across his dirty shirt front.

Rich Turnbull's first killing had stirred in him no feeling at all. This one was different. Riding away, Rich experienced a heady feeling of power — unbridled power. He laughed, liked the sound of it, and laughed again. The flat desert took the sound, carried it in shimmering, distorted waves away from him, and dropped it uneasily.

Before Rich reached the distant wall of rimrock that marked the boundaries of Salt Creek Plateau, black specks were wheeling and screaming high above Leo Trott's desert ranch. Looking back, Rich thought: *By nightfall they'll be on him. By this time tomorrow there won't be enough left to tell what happened.*

Chapter Ten

On Wednesday morning Lewt Grimes began his task of spreading the word up and down Salt Creek that Dayton Roark had called a meeting of the homesteaders for Thursday night. It was for the purpose of considering steps that might be taken in the future to protect the homesteaders' herds from the depredations of the Turnbulls.

In a sense, this amounted to an open declaration of war, and in some of the homesteaders it stirred feelings of uneasiness, in others downright fear. Lewt ran into varying reactions. At the place just out of town where young Petey Ritter lived, he found neither uneasiness nor fear, but only the outraged indignation of people at the end of human endurance onto whom has been piled more in the way of tribulation.

George Ritter, straightening more than he had for a year and perhaps conscious of his wife's eyes upon him, told Lewt: "You're damned right, I'll be there. Ain't things tough enough without the Turnbulls trying to make them tougher? How you going to stop 'em? What you figuring on doing?"

"Dayton says we can shove the cattle down onto Roark Ridge and put a guard on 'em."

Ritter nodded approvingly.

Lewt rode away. Ritter's wife went into the house, and Petey wandered barefoot down into the creek bottom. Ritter began the task of repairing a broken mower. Of late there had not been much thought in George Ritter as he worked, but today was different. He kept thinking of the four head of dry milch cows he had atop the plateau, and he kept thinking of the Turnbulls. He began to be aware that a full four days would elapse before the homesteaders could begin their roundup, and in four days the Turnbulls could easily dispose of a good many of the homesteaders' cattle.

Just before noon, George Ritter carefully put away his tools and walked to the house. He met his wife as she came through the door, carrying a basket of freshly washed clothes. He said perhaps a little hesitantly and waiting for her outspoken approval: "They'll meet tomorrow night. It'll take a full day to get ready, and another to get up on top of the mountain. That gives the Turnbulls four days. What do you think they'll be doing them four days? Sitting around the house?"

Impatience touched her voice. "What do I care what they'll be doing? I'm busy." She moved past him, heading toward the clothesline, and then she stopped. She stood utterly still for a moment, facing away from him. Then she turned. Anger that was touched with madness flushed her face. She said, her voice still and strained: "You're thinking about Molly and Babe and Jersey and Bess. They better not hurt them. They just better not."

Ritter said: "I thought maybe I'd go up there. I could try and find 'em, and, if I did, shove 'em on down with Dayton's stuff."

"You couldn't find 'em . . . not all by yourself."

He shook his head affirmatively. "I think I could. They have never drifted far from where I left 'em. They're not like range cattle." His voice turned decisive. "I'm going to try, anyhow."

He turned away, conscious of her stare against his back. Down in the bottom he caught one of his work horses, the lightest one, a smoothly muscled black. In the barn, he threw up his old saddle and cinched it down. He rode out with a wave toward his wife, but stopped as she ran toward him.

Her face, so lined and harsh, held something as she approached that made him remember what she had been like the first year of their marriage. It lost this quality as she came closer, became the face he had grown used to. Her voice, sharper even than usual, said: "You be careful, George! Hear me? You be careful!"

"Sure, hon."

There was understanding in George Ritter, understanding and bitterness because of the harshness of this life that made necessary the shell his wife wore. Riding past her, he leaned from the saddle and kissed her cheek. Color ran into her face for an instant, and then she frowned, turned away, and walked swiftly back toward the house.

George was a mile up the road before he realized that he had not thought of food. Neither had he brought a rifle. So when he came abreast of Lewt Grimes's tidy small cabin, he turned in.

Lewt came to the door at his hail, causing in George Ritter the twinge of pity he always felt at the sight of Lewt, but this did not show in George's face as he said sheepishly: "I'm going up on the mountain, but I came away without grub, and I forgot my rifle. I wonder if you'd let me take yours?"

"Sure, I'll get it." Lewt hesitated a moment, finally saying: "You're worried about your cows, but you hadn't ought to go up there alone the way things are. Wait until everybody gets together on it."

"That'll be three, four days." George shrugged. "I guess I'll go. I guess I'd worry too much if I didn't."

Lewt stared at him for a moment. "I got some biscuits. I'll wrap them in a gunny sack, and you can tie them on behind your saddle. Eating meat and nothing else gets kind of old."

He was back shortly, carrying his old rifle and a rolled-up gunny sack. George got down, tied the sack behind his saddle, and then tied the rifle on beneath his right stirrup.

The sun's heat beat squarely down upon him as he turned out the gate, scorching through his thin shirt. Dust rose behind him in a thin plume that settled quickly in the still air. He rode past the broad, green 3R meadows, smelling the sharp, pleasant odor of newly cut hay. Although the 3R was not yet half done with their haying, already there were eight or ten stacks dotted across the fields, their tops browned as nicely as those of fat loaves of bread. In the distance across the creek, George could see the crew, raking and stacking, could hear their faint shouts, and the clang of metal against metal as the rakes dumped.

He went on with the impression Dayton Roark's busy and peaceful outfit had made creating a pleasant feeling within him. Until he thought of the Turnbulls, of the way they looked at a man as though he was not a man at all, but just some kind of varmint that needed killing or driving away.

The afternoon wore away with George Ritter steadily riding, for a long while on the road, and finally on the trail that led up to the top of Salt Creek Plateau. He saw no riders, and he saw no game. At sundown, he came out on top, turning away from the trail and heading directly down the draw that led to Vince Brewer's camp. George Ritter, being one of the homesteaders who ran cattle up here, also paid his share of Vince's wages, and he intended to ask Vince's help in finding his cows.

Three hundred yards from Vince's camp, in a deep pocket of aspen, a deer bounded up, leaping away with ten-foot, stiff-legged jumps. George scrambled from his horse and with steady fingers untied the rifle. The horse pulled away from him and moved deeper into the brakes, reins trailing. George flung the rifle to his shoulder and loosed his shot. The deer, hit in mid-air, crumpled to the ground at the end of his leap. George ran to him, fishing in his pocket for his knife.

"By golly, I'll eat anyhow. I was beginning to wonder if I'd see any deer. Reckon Vince'll be along directly to see what the shooting was about."

He cut the deer's throat, then swiftly and methodically began to dress and skin the animal. At dusk he came into Vince's camp with the deer slung across his saddle and found the place deserted.

It was a feeling he could not rationalize, the uneasiness that stirred in him at finding the camp empty. But then he thought of Vince's liking for liquor and spoke to himself aloud. "He's gone to Salt Creek to get drunk. Damn him, anyway! Why don't he stay up here and do what he's paid to do?"

Chapter Eleven

George Ritter built a fire and fried a chunk of venison nearly as big as the skillet, eating ravenously this and the biscuits Lewt had given him. He found some coffee and a smoke-blackened pot, and, when this was hot, he drank the scalding liquid gratefully. Afterward, he carefully quartered the deer and hung it out on a pole Vince had rigged between two spruces for just that purpose.

I'll take it home with me, he thought, remembering how well Petey liked fresh venison that was scarce down in the valley at this time of year. He let the fire die out and, when it had become reduced to a bed of glowing coals, rolled himself in Vince's blankets and went to sleep.

He was up at dawn and fried another piece of venison. Then, mounting, he headed up out of the draw. There was beauty in this high country of a chill early morning not found in more arid Salt Creek Valley. The soil underfoot was rich and black, and grass and wild flowers grew here in rank profusion.

There were two men in the clearing around the spring, mounted men, and one, even at a distance of two hundred yards was plainly the top-heavy, hulking Rich Turnbull. Not fifty yards from the spring lay a cow, a brown-spotted Guernsey cow that George Ritter recognized immediately as the one his wife called Molly.

He heard a voice now, carrying clearly on the still air. "Damn it, Rich, I don't like this! Stealing cattle is one thing, and I can understand that. Shooting 'em . . . well, hell, it just ain't right."

Rich's heavy body came around as he turned his horse. His voice, full of unpleasantness and menace, said: "While you're working for me, you'll do what I tell you to do. You want to make something of that?"

Ritter's surprise and the instinctive caution and carefulness of a man who knew the face of failure well now gave way to wild and unreasoning rage. He broke from cover of the thicket, running awkwardly, yelling violent and bitter curses. Fifty yards from the pair he halted and brought the gun to his shoulder. He thumbed back the hammer and let it fall. The gun made a dead and harmless click.

George remembered then the deer he had

shot, remembered that he had forgotten to reload. He fumbled in his pocket for a cartridge. Rich Turnbull brought his Colt slowly and carefully to eye level and thumbed back the hammer. Ritter dived to the ground, but there was no cover here, and even the grass had been cropped short by the cattle that came to the spring to drink and lingered long enough to strip the surrounding area of feed.

Still fumbling in his pocket, George waited for the bark of Rich's revolver, for the smashing jolt of the bullet into his body. The 'puncher with Rich had drawn his own gun, and suddenly George Ritter quit his hopeless fumbling and stood up. If he had to die, he'd do it on his feet like a man, not like an animal, crawling on the ground.

Rich was an executioner, dispassionate and without feeling. He was in no hurry, apparently wanting his first shot to kill. The muzzle of his gun followed Ritter's every move patiently.

Suddenly the 'puncher who was with Rich raised his own gun, at the same time crowding his horse against Rich's. The muzzle of his gun made a sweeping downward arc, smashing against the wrist of Rich's gun hand. Rich howled with pain, and his gun dropped from nerveless fingers onto the ground.

He yelled: "Damn you, Amos! What the hell's the matter with you?"

Amos Leach's gun muzzle was steady and unwavering upon Rich's middle. His face had gone pale, and his eyes were unsteady with fear. But defiance was in him, too.

"You made a mistake, Rich. Everybody told you Amos Leach would do anything for his liquor, but that ain't quite true. There's places where even I draw the line. This is one of 'em."

"You're in this as deep as I am! If this sodbuster gets back to town, neither your hide nor mine ain't going to be worth much."

Amos shrugged. "My hide ain't worth much, anyway." He turned his glance to Ritter. "Move, mister. You'll get a half hour's start."

With a yell, Rich raked his horse, and the animal lunged against that of Amos Leach. Rich reached his long and powerful arms for the oldster, and he could have crushed him and broke his back with their power. But Amos brought his gun up, and its barrel descended against Rich's skull with an audible crack. Amos reined his horse away and watched as Rich slumped in his saddle and slowly slipped to the ground.

Without looking back, Amos rode to where George Ritter stood. His beard was red and unkempt. His hands shook, and his shoulders twitched. George suddenly recalled seeing him in Salt Creek, in various stages of drunkenness, but never sober.

Amos said wryly: "If you got a horse, mister, you better fork him and get the hell out of here. He ain't going to be pleasant when he wakes up."

"What are you going to do?"

"I'm heading to hell out of this country. By the time he wakes up, I'll be twenty miles from here. I can't beat him drawing, and I can't fight him. You think I'd stay around where he could get at me?"

George said in his slow and patient voice: "You saved my neck. Just thanks sounds kind of weak for that."

Amos Leach gave him a rueful grin, then whirled, and rode to Rich Turnbull's horse. He leaned to one side, catching the trailing reins, and rode out of the clearing leading the big man's horse. George Ritter gave the unconscious Rich a quick glance, then turned and disappeared into the timber.

Fear and a crowding panic were his trail companions that day. There is something about a killer who has no feeling when he kills that has a way of putting ordinary men at a disadvantage. George Ritter promised himself a dozen times that day — *Next time I see him, I'll shoot him down like I would a wolf.* — but each time his conviction lessened. At last, he knew it was not in him to kill any man in cold blood without giving him a chance. This left him but one alternative. Flight. For the law would give no ear to a sodbuster when he complained against a cattleman as powerful as Rich Turnbull.

Convincing Martha, his wife, when he turned up at their shack, was harder than convincing himself. "Leave?" she shrilled. "Not for the likes of him! He better not show his face around here! He just better not!"

Half convinced, George Ritter finally conceded: "Well, all right. I'll ride to town tonight. I'll spill my story at the meeting, and maybe then he'll have no reason for killing me."

All afternoon the rigs of the homesteaders filed past George Ritter's place. They came to Salt Creek in their wagons, in creaking buckboards and buggies. Some rode and some walked. But they all came.

Ritter went about his chores with lingering uneasiness. He could not forget the implacable calmness that had been in Rich

Turnbull, and the thought — *This is not over.* — kept turning in his mind. The rifle, loaded, was never far from his hand, although he doubted it would be of much use against Rich Turnbull's fast Colt.

Petey, tagging him, asked: "What'd he shoot Molly for, Pa? What's it like up there on the mountain? Is it like here? Whyn't you bring the buckskin home, Pa? Ma feels real bad about Molly, don't she, Pa?"

Ritter checked the impatience that stirred him at the boy's unending questions. He rumpled Petey's uncut hair. "You looked at the head gate today, son? Ain't much water coming down. You git up there and throw the weeds out of the head gate."

He watched the boy go through the fence, and his face softened as he saw Petey bend and retrieve his boat from its hiding place.

He ought to have real toys, he thought. *A boy's a man in this country too damned soon. I got to let him play more.* And he resolved that he would not scold Petey tonight no matter how late the boy straggled in.

Martha called him for supper as the sun lowered reluctantly behind the spruce-sprinkled rim, and, as he went into the house, she asked peevishly: "Now where'd you send that boy? You knew I was fixing supper early, so's we could go to the meeting."

"Up to the head gate."

He heard the pound of hoofs coming down the lane from the Salt Creek road half a mile away. Snatching up the rifle, he stepped to the door and outside into the soft-warm dusk that lay in the valley like a mist.

A shot crashed out as George Ritter stepped down off the stoop, before he had quite time to make out who his visitors were, or why they had come. As though struck by an invisible fist, Ritter doubled, dropped his rifle, and staggered. The will in him brought him straight again, his face twisted with pain and with hate.

Martha's sharp cry — "What is it, George?" — he cut short with his tight and roughly spoken: "Get in the house! Get back!"

Then his life was gone, and with it the will to stand straight. He folded onto the hard-packed ground without another sound.

Tonight, Petey waded downcreek from the head gate, sailing the boat ahead of him. The current here was faster than in the ditch, and it was this, perhaps, that put him within sight of the house as the raiders rode in.

Flood had washed these creek banks to perpendicular cliffs of clay, towering above his head for thirty feet. In spots, however, where the creek had changed its course, it left brushy half levels between field and creek that sloped gradually to the upper level of the fields. It was through one of these brushy pockets that Petey came, to stop abruptly at its edge as a shot rolled sharply toward him from the house.

For a long moment he stared at the milling riders, saw his father facing them, and no feeling stirred in him but that of curiosity. When his father croaked his tortured — "Get in the house! Get back!" — the strangeness of the scene began to impress itself upon Petey. As his father spilled onto the ground, terror laid its cold hand against Petey's heart.

What happened then was engraved forever in his brain. His mother, screaming and sobbing all at once, ran from the house to fall beside his father.

From one of the milling riders came an uneasy voice — "Let's get out of here." — to be silenced by Rich Turnbull's heavy, sneering: "Shut up!"

Seconds only the tableau took. It seemed to Petey like hours. His mother rose from his father's body, her weeping stilled, to stand for what seemed an eternity, unmoving. Like a tigress, then, she sprang for the fallen rifle. Her movements were those of a cat, swift and sure. She flung the rifle to her shoulder.

Rich Turnbull, easily distinguishable because of his top-heavy size, seemed not to move at all. But flame shot from his hand, once, twice, a third time. And Martha Ritter, with only a soft moan, sank across the body of her husband.

The uneasy voice raised in panic: "Damn you, Rich, what'd you have to do that for?"

Rich whirled his horse to face the voice, the half dozen riders who had so quickly turned against him. His own voice was cruel and harsh. "I did it because I had to do it! She'd've killed me. Now that it's done, don't a damned one of you forget that you're as guilty as I am. Don't go blabbing, or you'll hang with me."

Unconvinced, another man said: "You didn't have to kill 'em. You said you was going to give 'em their walking papers, not kill 'em."

Rich was vicious, and there was no pliancy in him. "He saw me shoot one of his cows up on the mountain. He'd've talked about that. I had to shut him up. Besides that, boys, this will put the fear of God into the damned sodbusters. Tomorrow you'll see 'em lined out on that road heading out of here. The grass'll be mine again. I'll tear down every damned fence and burn every damned shack in the valley! It'll grow back to greasewood and grass!"

Chapter Twelve

From his hiding place, Petey had risen and stood now in the open. He was surprised to find a rock clutched tightly in each hand. Terror and rage fought together for control of his stringy body.

"I'll kill him!" he raged through tight-set lips, but the voice of terror answered: *What with . . . rocks? He'll do to you just what he did to your ma and pa.*

Rich Turnbull rode from the yard, his men following and muttering behind him. When all sound of them was gone from the darkened yard, Petey ran for the house.

With tears running unashamedly down his dirt-stained and freckled cheeks, he shook his mother frantically, then his father.

"Ma! Pa! Get up! Pa, make her get up. Please, Pa, make her get up!"

He stayed until he began to feel the cold as it crept into their bodies. Terrified, then, he ran. He ran down Salt Creek in the dark, splashing barefooted through the water. He ran until he was altogether exhausted, and at last he stumbled and fell against a grassy bank. It was there he slept while the meeting of the homesteaders went noisily on in the town of Salt Creek.

Twisted little Lewt Grimes, his timidity gone, brought the meeting of homesteaders to order by thumping the butt of Dayton's pistol on the table. There was symbolism in this, indicating that peace was gone in Salt Creek Valley, and it stilled their talk immediately.

Lewt said, his voice strong: "This meeting's Dayton's idea, so I'll let him talk. Most of you have finished proving up on your homesteads, and have got your patents to the land. You think the hard times are over, but they ain't. Emil Turnbull rustled my cattle and sold 'em over in Utah, and the sheriff laughed at Day and me when we asked him to do something about it. You'll have a part of deciding what's to be done, but the way I feel about it is this. I've put a lot of work, all the money I had, and five years of my life into Salt Creek Valley. I ain't leaving!" He sat down.

Murmurs rose in the crowded room, the murmurs of men who are only half in agreement. Dayton rose to his feet. He shouted over this low noise: "There'll be talk that I'm using you to do my fighting. In a sense, it will be true. My motives in keeping all of you here are mostly selfish, because I need the hay you raise. Emil didn't take Lewt's cattle because he needed money. He figured Lewt would leave, if he lost his cattle. He figured it'd be too tough for Lewt to make a living off his hay alone."

"What's Lewt's troubles got to do with us?" The shouted question came from the rear wall of the room.

Day said patiently: "Lewt was the first, but he won't be the last. You'll all lose cattle if something isn't done."

Now again at the rear of the room a disturbance arose, in loud and indistinguishable voices as the door opened and a man came in. The man came down the aisle between the rows of seats, stopped ten yards from Day, and yelled: "I came by George Ritter's place to see if he was coming. He's laying in the yard, dead, and his wife's laying across his body. She's dead, too."

"What happened?" Day's question was echoed a dozen times throughout the room. There was a chill of horror stealing through his body as though he knew what the answer would be.

"They was shot. Missus Ritter had three bullet holes in her. George was shot in the chest. They was tracks of half a dozen horses in the yard!"

The man was sweating and out of breath. Every man in the hall came to his feet.

Day shouted: "Anybody know anything that might give us an idea of what happened, or why they were killed?"

Lewt leaned toward him. Day could hardly hear him because of the noise. Lewt said: "George came by my place yesterday and borrowed my rifle. He was going up on the mountain to look for his cows. I seen him go by again this afternoon, but he was traveling so fast he didn't stop to return the rifle."

Day raised his hand for quiet. The homesteaders had left their seats and were crowded around the man who had brought the news, a short, grizzle-bearded man whose name was Otto Hoff. The hall teemed with indignant noise.

Day yelled: "Hey! Listen!" When a measure of quiet had again been restored, he went on: "Lewt says George got worried about his cows yesterday after Lewt had talked to him about this meeting, and went up on the mountain. He borrowed Lewt's rifle. He was in a hurry, when he came back this afternoon, and didn't stop to return it. He must've seen something up on the mountain and was killed to shut him up."

A man in the crowd yelped: "What are we waiting for? Let's go get 'em! Let's get them murdering Turnbulls!"

Day had wanted support. He did not want a lynch mob. Neither did he want to precipitate a range war. His shouts brought no attention from the homesteaders, whose tempers were rising as flames rise through dry shavings. In desperation, Day raised his gun and fired at the ceiling. The shot brought instant silence, and he wasted no time in using it.

"We've got no proof that the killing was done by the Turnbulls! If it was, it's a case for the sheriff."

Catcalls answered this. "Yah! The sheriff! What will he do?"

"In a case of murder he'll have to do something. Let it go tonight, and tomorrow we'll look around and find out what it was that Ritter saw up there. Another bunch of you can try your hand at following the tracks out of Ritter's yard."

Lewt, seeming to gain stature, yelled: "I need half a dozen men to help bring the Ritters to town. Somebody ought to ride for the sheriff. Let's cut out the fight talk till we're sure what we're fighting."

Men came forward to volunteer, among them Otto Hoff. The meeting began to assume a belated order. Lewt and his half dozen left with a spring wagon for the Ritters' bodies, and a man mounted Day's horse for the ride to Glenwood Springs.

At ten, the meeting broke up, but as the wagons filed up the Salt Creek road, the temper of the homesteaders seemed to undergo a strange change. There was fear in them all as they drove into the dark, and the courage that comes to a man in a crowd evaporated. The voices of the women were sometimes shrill and scolding. Day heard one as he walked toward the center of town.

"John," she said to her husband, "we ain't going to stay and be murdered like the Ritters was. We're leaving. There ain't no land in the world worth getting killed over, least of all the land we're on."

Day walked the length of town toward the livery stable, for his horse had gone with the messenger to Glenwood Springs and he needed another. A light in the parlor of Kate Bradshaw's house made him pause there momentarily, thinking of this girl, wanting to see her. After only a slight hesitation, he went up the gravel walk and knocked.

Kate came to the door, a robe about her. Day said with embarrassment: "Never mind, Kate. I forgot it was so late."

"Bosh! Come in. Roxie and I were just

talking and wondering what happened at the meeting. Dad hasn't come home yet."

"Roxie? I thought . . . ?"

Kate's soft eyes cautioned him. She murmured: "Roxie is staying with me for a while."

Roxie sat on the sofa, also robe-clad, her feet tucked up under her. She smiled at him hesitantly. Seeing her brought the reminder to Day that he had not seen Tom since Monday night. Uneasiness troubled him for an instant until he saw Kate watching him, her expression grave.

He said: "I'm glad she decided on that."

Kate eased the tension by asking: "What happened at the meeting?"

"You haven't heard anything? Nothing at all?"

Kate shook her head. "Day, what is it?"

"The Ritters were killed. Both George and his wife. Shot down tonight in their yard."

Horror and incredulity drained Kate's face white. But Roxie was on her feet instantly and across the room. She clutched Day's arms, her fingers digging in with their insistence.

"The boy? What about the boy?"

Day was slow to comprehend. Then he recalled the Ritters' boy, Petey. This, then, was the odd apprehension in the back of his mind that had lingered there ever since Otto Hoff had brought the news. A new train of thought brought words tumbling from his mouth.

"Good Lord! I forgot him! They wouldn't dare!"

Roxie's eyes were wide with horror.

Day said: "No. Don't worry about it." And wondered briefly why Roxie should be so concerned over a boy she had never even seen.

Kate broke in now, thinking apparently that Day's words expressed his own thought, showing no realization that they were only to reassure Roxie.

"Day, if they'd shoot down a woman. . . . We've got to find that boy. We've got to find him before the Turnbulls do."

Day turned. "I'll find him."

"Wait. I'm going with you." Kate spoke first, and Roxie echoed her words.

Day shook his head. "You two can't ride around all night."

"Oh, can't I? You just watch me." Kate's mouth was firm. "If he saw the killing, he's the only one who did. Whoever did it is sure to realize that Petey is a noose around his neck."

Roxie asked, her voice turned hesitant

and shy: "Could I go too, Day? I've only seen Petey once, but. . . ."

Kate replied: "Doctor Slade said. . . ." She stopped.

Day looked from one to the other, puzzled.

Roxie's face mirrored her disappointment, but she shrugged lightly and forced a smile. "I guess you're right."

Kate ran from the room and in less than five minutes was back, dressed in blue jeans and jacket. Day grinned at the subdued Roxie, his puzzlement over the reason she could not go showing plainly in his face.

He said: "We'll find the boy. Don't worry."

Kate went out, and Day followed. The town was quiet now, and, as they passed down the street, lights began to wink out. At the livery barn, Day found the hostler still up, and ten minutes later he and Kate rode out of town on two hired horses.

"Why all the mystery talk back there between you and Roxie?" he asked. "Why couldn't she go?"

Darkness concealed Kate's face, but there was laughter in her voice. "Because she's going to have a baby, you dunce."

For a moment Day was silent, considering this. Then: "Does Tom know?"

"No. Roxie herself didn't know until Saturday night."

Chapter Thirteen

Jogging on, Day and Kate rode in silence for a while. Dayton cut through the greasewood until he struck the bed of Salt Creek, then turned along the cattle trail that wound upstream along the bank.

He said: "There will be riders on the road, maybe some Turnbull riders. Going this way, we won't be seen."

Kate snorted politely. "I hope you're not thinking what I think you are."

"What?"

"That Roxie's baby isn't Tom's. It is."

Day felt on the defensive. He had momentarily considered this possibility, but had rejected it guiltily. "I didn't say it wasn't."

"See that you don't." Kate dropped the subject quickly then, saying: "How far is the Ritter place?"

"Couple of miles. Maybe a little more, going this way."

While still a mile from the Ritters' fence, he cautioned her to silence. "Turnbull might be prowling around." Alertness and readiness came to him, and he wished he had been firm in refusing Kate. A man had no way of knowing what he'd run into on a ride like this.

Stars put a faint shine upon the surface of Salt Creek, showing its twisting, winding path. Willows grew thick here in the bottoms, and once Dayton halted, his hand dropping to his gun, as a startled deer crashed away ahead of them.

Another five minutes passed. Finally Day dismounted, whispering to Kate: "The horses make too damned much noise. Let's tie them up and go on afoot."

Walking carefully, they continued. Day felt extraordinarily jumpy and sought in his mind for the cause. Noises, small noises, rustled through the thicket, noises that could have been made by any small animal, or by a stealthy man. A twig cracked sharply a dozen yards ahead. Day, breathing softly, put out a restraining hand toward Kate's arm.

Suddenly a voice called softly up ahead: "Here he is, Rich. Sound asleep."

"Grab him, you fool!"

Day heard the crashing sound of a man moving through the tangle. There was the sound of a scuffle, a shrill boy's cry, and then the sound of running — fast. A shot bloomed in the blackness ahead, its racket deafening and startling in the nearly utter quiet.

"He got away!"

"We'll catch him, you damned bungler!"

Day was moving now, moving ahead, gun in hand. Kate stood frozen behind him. A shape darted from the blackness, nearly colliding with Day. His brawny hand shot out, collared the boy.

He whispered urgently: "Petey. Quit fighting. It's Dayton Roark and Kate, your teacher."

Suspicion kept the struggle in Petey until he heard Kate's soft voice. "Petey, it's all right. We won't hurt you. Be quiet, now."

He subsided then, panting hoarsely. Day said in a hushed tone: "Run with him, Kate. I'll hold them here."

She did not argue or hesitate. He heard them moving behind him, heard Rich's shout: "There he goes! Hear him?"

Day yelled — "That ain't Petey! It's me!" — and fired at the sound of crashing brush.

He dived to one side, cat-quick, as he fired. It was well he did. Bullets laced through the brush where he had been standing, but now he had a target. Swiftly and without consciously sighting he snapped two shots at the flash on his right, one at the flash on his left, and then he moved again, stooping low and running.

A twig, bullet-cut, fluttered from above his head and brushed his face. He stopped abruptly, quieting his breathing with a conscious effort. Behind him he heard the quick-running hoofs of the horses as Kate fled with Petey to safety.

To cover this noise, which he could only hope Rich had not yet heard, he spaced his remaining two shots, firing the second as the echoes of the first dwindled into nothing. Thumbing cartridges from his belt and pushing them into the loading gate of his Colt, he ran, making no effort at all to be quiet. He drew a fusillade of shots from Rich and his companion, and one of the bullets tore through his shirt and burned his back. Blood trickled from this, in a matter of seconds soaking his shirt and making it cling stickily to his back.

In the ensuing silence, Day strained his ears but could hear no sound behind him, no thudding of hoofs or crackling of brush. He sighed softly, and began his retreat.

He flung a stick first, far to his right, and blasted four times at the shots that sought out the noise. Dropping to the ground then, he waited out the bullets that answered his own shots, thinking when silence again blanketed the bottoms: *Guns empty.*

Cautiously he rose, and foot by foot felt his way back toward town. Behind him was only silence as Rich waited for him to show his position.

Nearly out of earshot, and hurrying now, Day heard Rich's conciliatory call — "Dayton, let's call this off!" — and grinned wryly. He covered nearly a quarter mile after this before he heard Rich's enraged bellow, dim with distance: "He's gone! Damn it, he's slipped away!"

Now, Dayton realized, the dangerous part of this game of hide and seek would begin. Rich, and whoever was with him, would mount and take to the road where the going would be fast. Dayton himself, afoot, had no chance whatever of beating them to town.

Reasoning as he traveled, he cut across a level patch of high greasewood, higher than a man's head when he sat astride a horse. Its spines clawed at him, tore his clothes, and scratched his face and hands. The bullet burn on his back smarted and pained and bled anew.

He reached the road, panting and out of breath, and stopped for an instant to listen, forcing his ragged breathing to quiet. Up the road he heard the pounding beats of a pair of horses, echoed from something so that oddly it sounded as though horses were coming from both directions.

I'll drop their horses out from under them as they go by, he thought, and eased back into the covering greasewood to wait.

The beat of hoofs came closer, but he realized that it was no echo that came to his ears from the direction of town. It was another pair of horses, and they would meet Rich and his companion near the place where Day now hid.

Kate? he wondered. *She hid the boy out somewhere and came back for me.*

He yanked his Colt from its holster and hastily checked the loads. Upcreek the dim shapes of Rich and his rider clattered into sight, and Day raised the gun, loosing three shots in quick succession. One of the horses grunted and rolled end over end. A man, flung clear, hastily crabbed away into the greasewood. The other horse, checked so sharply that he slid in the dusty road on his haunches, came erect, whirled, and ran back a hundred yards before melting into the greasewood.

Day moved downcreek in the gloom of starlight, keeping the high brush at his back, and traveling slowly and cautiously in the deep dust. He had gone perhaps two hundred yards when he glimpsed the dark shapes of horses against the sky.

He called softly: "Kate?"

"Here, Day. Hurry!"

He touched her shoulder briefly, squeezing, before he swung up to the saddle. She went ahead of him, running, and behind them a harmless, helpless shot banged in chagrin.

A few moments later, out of earshot of Rich, Day yelled: "Where's Petey?"

"I turned him loose at the edge of town and told him to go to my place."

They came into town, trotting the blowing horses, and pulled up before Dan Bradshaw's neat frame house. The shades were drawn, but light showed around their edges. Day swung down, and lifted a hand to help Kate. For an instant he thought she would refuse it, but then she took it and slipped to the ground.

It was in him to say: *Nice work, Kate. No man could have done better.* But there was something about the way she stood, something about the lifted paleness of her face that stopped him.

She swayed against him and suddenly she was tightly in his arms, her body warm and eager against his. He dropped his lips to her face, tasted the saltiness of tears, and then found her lips, parted and fierce. Timeless and rousing was this kiss, and, when it was done, he whispered hoarsely: "Katie, Katie, why did I wait so long?"

Her body still molded and fitted tightly against him, she murmured, gently mocking: "That's what I have wondered. But the waiting is over now."

Chapter Fourteen

The scene in the Bradshaw parlor was one of apparent peace and contentment. Roxie sat in a corner of the sofa, and beside her was Petey, bathed and scrubbed, clad in Dan Bradshaw's outsize pajamas. In Roxie's hands was a book, and in her voice, as she read, and upon her face was a tranquility Day had never seen in her before.

Clashing with the contentment of the scene was Dan Bradshaw, his chair tilted against the wall, a shotgun across his knees, and there were still traces of his fear and bereavement in Petey's freckled face. Dan came upright, the question on his lips: "Did they follow you?"

Day shook his head. "Dropped a horse from under one of them. It was Rich, all right, but he's the sheriff's job now. Emil would have gone along, playing it slow and safe, and might have won out in the end. But not Rich. He's too hotheaded and hates too strongly to play it that way."

Roxie looked up, smiling, and nodded toward the heavylidded Petey. "This boy belongs in bed. We all do. Time enough tomorrow to worry about Rich Turnbull."

Kate and Roxie and Petey disappeared into the back of the house. Day regarded Dan Bradshaw for a moment. "I'll sleep here on the sofa," he suggested. "Rich is like a mad dog and liable to do anything. Even as a kid, when he got an idea into his head, he didn't know where to draw the line."

Dan nodded, yawning. He scratched his head, his reluctance to go plain.

Day grinned then, thinking of Kate. He said: "You'll be lonesome without Kate, but you've had her long enough."

"Glad to get rid of her. She nags a man."

The older man's mouth was wide with a shameless grin. He knocked out his pipe, unbuttoned his shirt, and slouched with satisfaction from the room.

Kate came in almost immediately after, a basin of water and bandages in her hands. "What did you do to that back? Scratch it on the greasewood?"

"Bullet."

Putting the basin down, Kate's face was soft with compassion, as she came to Day. He caught her arms.

"Just burned it. Right now this is more important." He pulled her close and kissed her. "You know this could get to be a habit . . . if I don't try to stop."

"Don't stop. Don't ever stop, Day."

She pulled loose, turned him gently, and tore his shirt away from the wound. Water upon it made it smart, but her hands were gentle and soon had the wound bandaged.

He kissed her again, but again she pulled away from him. "Day, I'm shameless, but if you do that again, I won't be able to leave this room."

"When will you marry me, Kate? Right away?"

"You know I will. Whenever you say."

She gave him a smile and slipped from the room. Day blew out the lamp and lay down on the sofa. The fatigue of the last several days let him think of Kate for only a moment. Then he slept.

Daylight brought a gray overcast to the skies that, before breakfast was over, had lowered and turned to cold, drizzling rain. The dust on the Salt Creek road turned quickly to mud, a slippery, clay-like mud that clung to a man's feet until it weighted them down with huge, clinging gobs. But the wagons came through the rain and mud, the homesteaders' wagons, some of them loaded for the trip out of the Salt Creek

138

country, and some of them carrying only their occupants.

Trouble has a way of bringing men together, for in company there is security. As they gathered in knots in town, shoulders hunched against the rain, the temper in these men rose, and their talk turned ugly. In Salter's store the women gathered, their indignation making a buzz of noise down the length of the long room.

Lewt Grimes came to town astride his bony black, hauling up before Day where he stood under the awning in front of the bank.

" 'Morning, Dayton."

Day grinned, the grin taking all grimness from his rain-splashed face. " 'Morning, Lewt."

A knot of men gathered around these two, and finally one of the homesteaders asked: "Are we going to mill around town all day? Ain't there something we can do about the Turnbulls?"

Day said: "The sheriff will be in on the train this afternoon. I reckon the Ritters' funeral will be put off till tomorrow, as long as it's raining so hard today. Ain't much a man can do."

Lewt asked: "What you figure Rich is up to now?"

Day shrugged. He had been wondering

the same thing himself. He had been trying to fathom the workings of Rich Turnbull's mind from what he knew of the man. That Rich was vicious, he had known since he was a boy in school. But now his thought was that there must be a touch of madness in anyone who could murder a man and woman because they were homesteaders, and hunt down a seven-year-old boy as though he were a coyote. If there was madness in Rich's mind, then there was no telling what he might do.

At nine, Tom Roark came riding in, a canvas-wrapped bundle slung across a led horse trailing behind him. He halted before Day, and Day felt a stir of relief at seeing him.

He asked: "Where in the hell have you been? I haven't seen you since Monday night."

"Riding."

Lewt mumbled something about an errand and stepped away. Tom dismounted, moving under the shelter of the awning, still holding the reins of his horse.

He said: "I had to think things out. I went up on the mountain and camped." He gave Day a wry grin. "I've done a lot of thinking in the last three days."

The impulse was in Day to tell his brother that he had been wrong about Roxie, but he stopped himself with the realization coming to him at last that you do not help a man by smoothing his way. He asked: "What did you decide?"

"You'll think I'm a fool."

Day shook his head.

Tom was hesitant. "First I decided that I wanted Roxie no matter what she'd done, no matter even what she might do in the future."

Day waited.

Tom fought the words from his mouth. "After that, I got to thinking about Roxie and about Rich. I began to realize that in two years of living with Roxie, I'd got to know her damned little better than I did when I first met her. But Day, she's always been . . . well, kind of refined, you might say, and Rich is rough. He talks filthy, and he thinks filthy. I just don't think she could stand Rich near her."

"Why didn't you hunt Vince up, and find out what he really saw?"

"I did."

"What'd he say?"

"He couldn't say anything." Tom nodded his head toward the shapeless bundle that lay across the pack horse. In his face was revulsion and an almost physical sickness. "He's dead. He's mangled from falling off the rim and not very pretty. But he's got a bullet hole in him made by a rifle bullet with a soft nose. It tore a hole through him you could put your fist in."

Day felt a chill in his spine. Murder was ugly, and it had struck too many times. "Where'd you find him?" he asked.

"On the trail above the Turnbulls' house."

"Any tracks?"

"Sure. Lots of tracks. Too damned many to tell anything from."

The overcast had lifted somewhat, and the rain had slowed. A wind blew in from the northwest, bringing the smell of clean-washed earth and the sharp, pleasantly pungent smell of wet sagebrush. It also carried the homely smell of burning wood. Day turned his head upcreek, for a stove fire at this time of year was not usual. In the valley of Salt Creek lay a pall of smoke, held close to the ground by rain and by the heaviness of the air.

Day yelped: "So that's what Rich is doing."

Others had noticed this smoke. Along the rainy street rose an ugly, menacing rumble, the audible anger of men who have stood enough. Even those who had come to Salt

Creek that morning, packed to leave, joined in this.

Day shouted: "We need horses . . . saddle horses! Come down to the stable! I'll stand the hire on the horses!"

In ten minutes there were thirty men mounted, riding out of town at a full, hard run. Others, for whom there had not been saddle horses, followed astride their slower work and wagon horses.

Just at the edge of town, not more than a mile out, a log house was burning fiercely. A precious haystack smoldered nearby, turned black from the rush of flame over its outer dryness, and slowly being ruined entirely by the creeping smolder under its overhang.

Farther upcreek, another plume of smoke arose, and, farther still, a third. The rage in the riding men passed all bounds of control, and Day, while himself fully enraged by this wanton destruction, could still feel a touch of regret that he was riding at the head of such a lawless mob. They would tear Rich Turnbull to bits when they caught him; they would burn and destroy the Turnbulls' home ranch with the same fury that they destroyed Rich.

At each burning homestead, a few of the men dropped off to combat the fires. Rain came down in a steady drizzle that was more like mist than rain, and did little to help.

Finally, with but one fire burning ahead of them, they were forced to halt to rest the horses. Every one of these was sweated and breathing harshly. The flame of rage in the homesteaders had died from its first white heat, and now burned slowly and steadily.

Day dismounted, slipped the saddle from his horse, and rubbed the animal vigorously with the saddle blanket. Tom did the same for his mount, and in spite of the urgency the others, even in their fury, recognizing that a spent horse is useless, did likewise.

The horses cooled slowly, and their breathing became normal. Day squatted beside the road and rolled a smoke, sheltering it under a flap of his slicker. His eye wandered over something on the ground, passed on, and returned uneasily — a cigar, discarded by someone while it was less than half smoked, and not too long ago, for it was not yet thoroughly soaked.

Otto Hoff bellowed: "Let's go before the son-of-a-bitch fires another one!"

Day cinched down his saddle and rose to it. Tom stayed beside him and asked uneasily: "How you going to stop them once they get hold of Rich?"

"There'll be no stopping them. But we'll

have to try, because Rich's riders will stand and fight for him."

The presence of that half-smoked cigar lingered in the back of Day's mind, making him uneasy, although he did not know why. No homesteader could afford to smoke cigars, and, even if they could, they would never discard one half smoked.

Someone else must have stood there beside the road and . . . ? Suddenly, and with terrifying logic, the pieces of the puzzle began to fall into place in Dayton's mind. Rich Turnbull smoked cigars. He had a habit of tossing away the one he was smoking whenever he moved into action. Day recalled the half-smoked cigar Rich had tossed away when he had moved into the fight with Tom.

The fires, then, had not been set without purpose. The purpose behind them was to draw the men away from town, to leave Petey defenseless! Rich had waited here, watching.

Day yanked his horse to a halt.

Tom glanced over his shoulder at him, wondering, but reined back at the expression he saw in his brother's face. "What's the matter?"

"Come back here to where we stopped. I hope I'm wrong! Oh, Lord, I hope I'm wrong!"

Galloping, he reached the spot in an instant. It was atop a small rise of land and overlooked the entire valley below. Tracks led away from the road here, and Day followed them impatiently, unconscious of the wet brush against him. At a spot hidden in the brush, he found where Rich had tied his horse, saw Rich's boot tracks where they had dug deeply into the mud as he had mounted. Then the horse tracks led away downcreek, toward the town of Salt Creek.

"I was right! And Roxie and Kate are down there alone with Petey!"

With thundering disregard for the slickness of the road, scattering gobs of mud behind them, the two men raced down the road toward town, sparing neither spur nor quirt, for even horses were of no value when weighed against a human life.

Chapter Fifteen

Lewt Grimes, from a quarter mile away, saw the Roarks go with a touch of relief. Their leaving in such haste told him that they had reason to believe Rich Turnbull had sneaked back into town. Part of his relief was occasioned then by the knowledge that in all probability neither he nor the homesteaders would today be guilty of lynching Rich. It was further occasioned by the realization that Day, who would surely have tried to stop the homesteaders from violence, would now be relieved of that useless and thankless task.

Within his mind arose the inevitable conflict, for he knew that upon himself would fall the decision as to whether he should try and stop the burning of the Turnbull spread and thus earn the outright dislike of these men whose good will he valued so, or whether he should stifle his conscience and go along with them. There was no question in Lewt's mind but what the Turnbulls had earned whatever they would get today. But burning was a lawless thing and would forever leave its stain upon those who participated in it.

At the last fire, the owner and two others reluctantly broke away from the bunch to go and fight the fire. The remainder, now numbering between fifteen and twenty, rode on to the confluence of Dry Creek and Salt Creek, turning onto the narrower road that led to Emil Turnbull's trashy spread.

Lewt unwillingly voiced his protest, driven by some inner compulsion he could not control. "I ain't holding out for Rich, but this ain't the right way to settle things. There'll be killing, and, when it's all over, the law'll say we're as guilty as the Turnbulls."

Otto Hoff sneered: "Scared, Shorty?"

Lewt flushed painfully at the reference to his deformity. His jaw stiffened. "No, I ain't scared."

He wanted to tell them what was in his mind, that human society does not thrive upon lawless violence, that upon those guilty of violence must ever rest the stigma of it. But you do not reason thus with men whose minds are aflame with fury and with blood lust. Besides that, he could detect now, after his first tentative protest, a cooling of these men toward him, suspicion and plain dislike. Lewt Grimes lifted his twisted shoulders in a resigned shrug. The gesture said plainly that human passions cannot be changed or cooled with words.

The rain stopped entirely, and a chill wind blew down off the high mesa. For another half hour the sodbusters rode, and at last the sprawling and untidy Turnbull ranch came into sight. Riders, lounging in the yard, scurried out of sight like ants as the home-steaders came into view. When they reached the gate, a flurry of rifle shots popped in the Turnbulls' yard.

The homesteaders hesitated. A rifle spoke from the house, and Otto Hoff's horse reared and fell, kicking. Otto scrambled to his feet, muddy and limping. He yelled: "Get back in the brush! Circle the damned place!"

Another volley of shots sent the would-be raiders into the cover of high brush, but Lewt Grimes held his ground. Dismounted to present a smaller target, he shouted: "Hello, the house! You know what Rich done last night? He murdered the Ritters! Do you know what he done today? He burned homesteads from here to Salt Creek!"

He was hoping that these riders of the Turnbulls were no different from other men who were working for their thirty a month and beans. They would fight for their outfit because that is the way of a cowpuncher. But would they fight for a skunk like Rich, who had killed a defenseless woman, who had tried to kill a seven-year-old boy, her son?

Silence lay across the valley. Lewt gambled. "Ride out or walk out with your hands up!"

There was no sound at all from the place then for a full two minutes. Finally a man showed himself from behind the squat log barn. His hands were raised, and he walked hesitantly, as though still not fully decided in his own mind that this was right.

Lewt prayed silently that the homesteaders would hold their fire. As evidence of good will, he mounted and sat his horse astride the lane, ludicrously tiny and alone. More men came from hiding in the yard, their hands half raised, and began their shuffling march toward Lewt.

Suddenly, when they were nearly halfway to Lewt Grimes, a rifle spoke from the window of Emil Turnbull's sod-roofed house. Lewt Grimes was driven clear out of his saddle by the bullet's vicious impact, limp and sodden.

From the group of marching men arose roars of resentment, and, echoing it, came the wicked crack of rifles from the brush surrounding the house.

A yell came out of the brush: "Hit the dirt, or you'll get it, too!"

The Turnbull riders dropped out of the line of fire, crawling on their stomachs for the dubious shelter of the low brush that lined the road. Bullets whined over their heads and thudded into the ancient log walls of Emil Turnbull's house.

A dozen men on horseback charged out of the greasewood at the rear of the house, carrying flaming cedar torches. They swarmed around the house. In minutes, flames began to lick from the scrap lumber that Emil had so frugally stored against his ranch house.

The barn came next, then the tumble-down chicken house, the reasonably new bunkhouse. Emil Turnbull's shots cracked from the windows of the main house, but the concentrated hail of fire from the brush put a stop even to this.

At last, as flames caught in the dry and rotting logs, the door of the house opened, and Emil's wife came out, her face bitter and hating. She stood defiantly on the stoop for a moment, and, when she drew no fire, marched to the corral and caught a horse that she mounted astride. Walking the horse, and not looking back, she moved down the road toward the town of Salt Creek.

The fires mounted, and the homesteaders galloped in the yard to administer to the wounded and to stand appalled at what they had done. At last, herding the Turnbull riders before them, trailing a wagonload of dead and wounded behind, they began their ride back toward town.

In the town of Salt Creek, at a quarter after nine that morning, Dan Bradshaw had saddled his horse and ridden away from his house, taking the Salt Creek road in the wake of the infuriated homesteaders.

Kate had left soon after, heading downstreet toward Salter's store. Before leaving, she had told Roxie: "You'll be safe enough with Petey as long as Rich is busy setting fires. I ought at least to try to persuade the women to stay on in their homesteads. I hate to see them give up all they've worked for . . . everything they have in the world."

Roxie had been left alone then with Petey. The shock of the night before was beginning to wear away, leaving in the boy the full knowledge that he was now utterly alone. He was quiet, still of face, and his silence and tearlessness brought a choking tightness to Roxie's throat.

This morning, Roxie wore a bright print dress, full of skirt, that swished about her ankles as she walked, and held her tightly at waist and breast. The boy sat at one end of the long sofa, looking little and lost, and Roxie sat down close beside him.

"Would you like to have me read to you?"

He made his face brighten politely, but she could tell his thoughts were elsewhere. He asked: "You reckon I could get a job somewheres?"

"Boys your age have to go to school."

"How can I do that? I got to live somewheres, and I got to eat."

Roxie felt a burning sensation behind her eyes. She said softly: "I'd like to have you live with me, but maybe you wouldn't want to."

His face brightened instantly. "Sure I would. I'd like that fine. I could help. . . ." He halted. "Maybe Mister Roark wouldn't want me."

Helplessness tied Roxie's tongue momentarily, but then she murmured: "He couldn't help but want you, Petey." Wanting so to make a home for Petey, she thought — *I'll go to Tom and make him understand.* — and from her mind she brushed the doubts that rose to scoff at her determination. She made her smile reassuring. "It's settled, then?"

He nodded. "Would you read to me now?"

Roxie got the book of Mother Goose rhymes. She settled herself on the sofa beside him and began to read:

"I saw a ship a-sailing
A-sailing on the sea
And it was full of pretty things
For Petey and for me
There were comfits in the cabin
And apples in the hold. . . ."

Petey asked: "What's a comfit?"

"I'm afraid I don't know."

She waited a moment, and then went on. Her voice was soft and calm, but uneasiness that she could not understand began to build up in her. It started as an odd chill in her spine that crept through her body until she was clammy with cold. She began to think of Rich Turnbull, of his coarseness and viciousness, and she began to be afraid.

She closed the book, marking the place with a scrap of newspaper. "Just a minute, Petey. I'll build up a fire."

"I'm not cold. Don't stop now."

"I'll only be a minute." She went first to the front door and locked it. Then she went to the back. Returning, she shook the ashes down in the potbellied parlor stove and added paper and wood to it, standing for a moment to warm her back while it caught.

She told herself as the chill returned: *You're being silly. Rich Turnbull is ten miles up Salt Creek setting fires. There are twenty or thirty men after him. Do you think he'd risk coming into town?* She considered this for a moment, deciding with a quick increasing terror: *There are no men in town! They've all gone to fight the fires. There would be little danger for Rich in coming here.*

Petey asked: "Will you read some more?"

"All right."

She picked up the book and began to read, but the sentences blurred and made no sense. Forcing concentration, she continued:

"Who has seen the wind?
Neither I nor you;
But when the leaves hang trembling
The wind is passing through.

Who has seen the wind?
Neither you nor I;
But when the trees bow down their
**   heads,**
The wind is passing by."

Roxie shuddered violently. Suddenly she could read no more. The wind in the rhyme had abruptly assumed the identity of the unseen menace that hung over her and over Petey. Nervously she went to the window and stared out at the bleak gray landscape. From here she could see a bend in the road half a mile out of town, could see parts of it from there until it lost itself in the cotton-woods at the edge of town.

She stared at that bend in the road, her nervousness building until she was trembling. Petey, coming to stand beside her, asked: "What you looking at? Don't you feel good?"

She turned her head, trying desperately to smile reassurance at the boy. "I guess not, Petey. I was just looking at the rain."

"It ain't raining now. Can I go out for a while?"

"You stay with me until Kate comes home. Would you mind doing that?"

Petey must have answered, but Roxie did not hear him. A man was coming down the Salt Creek road, visible for an instant at the bend, and there was no mistaking him — a top-heavy man who towered over the horse he was riding, making the animal seem undersize. He was visible at the bend, but he disappeared then. Roxie did not see him again, although she watched the next visible stretch of road with horrified concentration.

Rich Turnbull, she knew, had left the road. That much was obvious. He was even now approaching, by devious trails, through the high greasewood, and he could have but one purpose in coming to Salt Creek.

Chapter Sixteen

Of a sudden, the insecurity of even these four walls oppressed Roxie. She wanted to open the door and run, to flee through the brush at the back of the house, to hide, to do anything but stay here, waiting, waiting. Panic caught at her and brought its chill of terror.

She thought of Kate, and for an instant her heart cried out: *Oh, Kate! Come back! Come back now!*

Petey's voice held alarm. "What's the matter? What's the matter with you?"

His fear for some unknown reason lessened her own, made her feel her responsibility toward him. She forced her voice to be calm. "There is someone coming, Petey. You are I are going to hide . . . and play a joke on them."

But the terror of last night was a thing too recent in the boy for him to be easily fooled. His chin quivered. "It's him, ain't it?" His face had gone dead-white. "We got to get out of here! We got to run!" His immature voice had risen to a near scream.

"He's got a horse, Petey." Roxie could have bitten off her tongue. She had not meant to admit Rich's presence to the boy.

"We can get a horse, too. Mister Bradshaw keeps two or three out in the barn. I seen 'em this morning. Come on, Miss Roxie! Please! Come on!"

Roxie thought: *If we could get to Salter's store, he wouldn't dare hurt us there where so many people could see.* But she shook her head. The minute they opened the door, they'd run right into Rich. She had no way of knowing where he was. She said firmly: "We're safe here. The doors are locked. Kate will be coming home soon."

A horse nickered beside the house. Roxie started violently and began to tremble. Something touched the frame north wall, perhaps Rich's holstered gun, scratching along it for an instant, and stopping.

A step sounded on the porch. Roxie drew Petey with her and crouched behind the sofa. A shadow darkened the window. Roxie dared to peep over the sofa and saw Rich's heavy body, his scowling brutal face. Again his steps sounded, spurs jingling, and the screen door opened. A heavy hand pounded against the door.

"Hey! Open up! You let me have that kid, honey, and I won't hurt you!"

Petey was trembling violently, and his teeth chattered.

Rich bellowed: "Open up, you damned little slut, or I'll kick the door down!"

Roxie whispered desperately: "Run out the back door, Petey, as quiet as can be. Slip a bridle on a horse and ride away real quiet. Then circle around until you can slip downtown without being seen. Go to Salter's store."

"I ain't going to leave you." His voice was small, but stubborn.

Rich's heavy boot crashed against the door.

Roxie screamed: "You'd better leave! Dayton and Tom will kill you!"

She heard his heavy laugh. "They're on a wild-goose chase up Salt Creek. They're twenty miles from here." His voice turned wheedling. "Come on now, open up. I ain't goin' to hurt you."

Roxie whispered, panic turning her voice sharp: "Petey, you go do what I tell you. Rich won't hurt me. It's you he's after. Go on now." She pushed him away from her. "I'll keep him here at the door, talking."

Suddenly the boy was gone. Roxie cried, hoping to cover the noise of his departure: "Dan Bradshaw and Kate are due back here now. You'd better go!"

Rage turned his voice harsh. "Like hell! I want that kid!" His heavy boot crashed against the door, again and again. It shivered from the blows but did not give.

Roxie laughed hysterically. "You can't kick it down! It's too strong for that!"

"The hell I can't." His kicks grew frenzied, harder. A screw popped out of one of the hinges and rolled along the floor. Roxie thought: *Another minute and Petey will be gone. Another minute! Oh, please give Petey another minute!*

The top hinge gave way, and a crack of light showed between door and frame at the top. Rich's boots sounded on the porch as he backed off. Roxie heard a stir behind her, jumped and whirled as a hand touched her arm.

Petey whispered: "I got two horses ready. Come on."

His thin body jumped and twitched, and his eyes were wide and wild. Roxie had never seen, hoped never to see again, such terror in a human being. She was on her feet and running with him through the house. Anger and exasperation stirred in her at his stubbornness, but it lasted only a moment, and then her dark eyes filled with tears. He had come back for her! He could have escaped, but he had come back!

As they reached the back door, the front gave with a crash of splintering panels. Rich's bellow shook the house. Furniture crashed as he overturned it, searching for them.

Then they were running down the walk and into the cool, damp stable. Roxie pitched Petey astride one of the horses, and opened the barn door. She clutched the mane of the other horse, her skirt startling him, and swung to his back as he jumped, running, through the door.

A shot racketed out, and the bullet buzzed like an angry bee past Roxie's ear. Then the brush was clawing at her as she crouched low on the neck of the galloping horse, following the twisting course through the greasewood where Petey led. Pain, like a taloned claw, clutched at her middle. Faintness overwhelmed her. She thought of Dr. Slade's words — "No horseback riding." — but galloped on, for death rode close behind.

A half mile out of Salt Creek, Kate Bradshaw, bareheaded and astride her speeding horse, met Dayton and Tom. With scarcely a slackening of speed, she circled and swept along beside them.

Out of breath, she cried: "He's been at the

house! The door's kicked down and the place is a wreck! Roxie's gone, Day . . . and Petey, too! I heard a shot as I was coming home, and hurried. Oh, Day, do you think . . . ?"

Day's face was bitter with self-blame. He had fallen for Rich's trap so easily — and now Roxie and Petey would pay for his stupidity if they had not already. He answered her with a helpless shrug.

The three swept into the turn just outside of town. Day's sharp eyes spotted the place where Rich had left the road, but he rode on, for there was a faster cutoff a little farther on. He reached this, and swerved his horse a little ahead of Tom and Kate now. In another minute, he skidded to a stop before the Bradshaw stable, read the tracks instantly, and quirted his jaded horse after them.

Erratically they led through the high brush, circling slowly toward the town. As quickly as it became apparent to Day that Roxie and the boy wanted to get into town, so had it become apparent to Rich, for his tracks left those of the two, cutting away toward town to intercept them.

Day shouted at Tom: "You two follow Roxie! I'll stay with Rich!" And he swerved along the single set of tracks without looking back.

He ran his horse along this route for a quarter mile, finding then where Rich had stopped and waited, finding where he had turned, apparently disappointed, toward the low, cedar-covered knoll behind the town.

Day felt a touch of hope. Roxie had not been so frightened that she had not been using her head. She had noted Rich's absence behind her, had guessed that he would cut off her trail, and try to intercept her. Discovering this, she had immediately changed her plan and had headed toward the knoll, hoping undoubtedly to conceal herself and Petey in the cedars until help could arrive.

Nearly to this knoll, Day cut her tracks and those of Kate and Tom, following. Ahead, suddenly, he heard Tom's shout: "Roxie! It's Tom! Where are you?"

Immediately he heard her answer faintly, to the right: "Here! Oh, hurry, Tom, hurry!"

A shot rolled flatly through the cedars, and then the sound of a horse crashing through them. Day, slowing his horse, heard then a woman's sobbing, her incoherent words: "Oh darling, I thought. . . . Oh, Tom!"

For just an instant, Day's face softened into a smile. Then, again, he cut the tracks of Rich's heavy, shod horse, and spurred along after the man.

These cedars, ancient and twisted, stretched their grotesque hands for a man riding through them. At times, they formed an impenetrable screen; at others, they thinned and let a man ride straight. Back into the wild, low hilly country led Rich's tracks. A wolf, running from the trail, turned to bare his fangs at Day. The thought ran through Day's head: *He can't be far ahead or I'd never have seen that wolf.*

Almost he missed the place where Rich had left his horse. The man had caught a low, overhanging limb of one of the cedars, but he had broken off a dead branch as he did. It lay across the trail, a sign that stirred the watchfulness in Day. Ten yards farther on, the horse had slowed, hesitated for an instant, and then gone on, but more slowly.

Abruptly fear laid its cold hand on Day. A few seconds only it had taken him to decipher the signs on the ground, but a few seconds was enough for an ambusher to draw a bead. Day flung himself from his horse, landing on hands and knees on the muddy ground. The explosion of a Colt roared ten yards to his right, and his horse reared and fell thrashing beside him. Dayton rolled to avoid the kicking hoofs, grateful for the protection the wounded horse afforded him.

As the animal's head came around, Dayton put a bullet into it, and the horse, after one last long shudder, lay still. Day's hands were covered with the slick adobe mud. Now his gun grips were also covered with it. He crawled close to the steaming horse, wiped his hands on its lathered side, wiped, too, the butt of the gun.

All sound had stopped in this cedar thicket except for the rustling of the trees as the moisture dripped from their branches. Day called, uneasy about his back — "Come out of there, Rich, your hand's played out." — and hoped for a sound that would betray Rich's position. He heard none.

Ten feet behind him was the thick-lichened trunk of a centuries-old cedar. He squirmed back, staying close to the ground, but wholly aware that before he reached it his entire body would be exposed to Rich. A bullet smacked into the mud beside his head, spraying him with the fine adobe clay. Day dived back behind the horse, raising almost immediately and poking his gun before him. Again a shot banged out, and this one burned the side of his head. But he had a target. Rich stood in a thick screen of branches, his face distorted and wholly savage, his eyes narrowed with wicked concentration.

Day took time to sight, almost too much time, for Rich ducked back. But Day's bullet, missing the man's chest, took him in the right shoulder. He yelled, an anguished yell of pain, and leaped into the open. His gun was dropping from nerveless fingers when Day's second shot took him square in the chest, driving him backwards in a grotesque, staggering shuffle. He sprawled on his back in the mud, lifeless, but even in death the viciousness, the wickedness remained in his heavy features.

Day looked at him for a moment, feeling nothing but relief, then started his walk toward town.

Riding double, with Kate's arms about his waist, Day Roark came back into Salt Creek in the early afternoon. The overcast was drifting away, and the sun shone through the rifts in the clouds, laying its warmth on the steamy landscape. They met young Doc Slade coming down the Bradshaw walk. He smiled at Kate's concerned expression, saying: "That young woman nearly lost her baby, but she's all right now."

Day swung Kate to the ground. There were tears in her soft gray eyes, tears of happiness. Petey came shuffling down the walk, and Day asked: "Where's Tom?"

The boy nodded over his shoulder. His obvious embarrassment told Day what he needed to know.

Day said: "Go down to that little gray house on the corner. Tell the preacher he's needed for a wedding. After supper I'll hire a surrey, and we'll all go home." He asked Kate: "Am I rushing you? I was thinking that tomorrow will see the start of the damnedest house-raising bee you ever saw."

Kate, her lips curving softly, shook her head, slipped her arm through Day's, and drew him toward the house. Petey watched them until they were inside, and then he turned. His freckled face tried hard to show his disapproval.

He snorted: "Mush! That's what it is, mush!"

But the sun was warm against his back, and after a while he began to whistle.

The Woman
at Ox-Yoke

Chapter One

Afterward, Dan Iles could look back and wonder how he could have been so foolish. But that was days afterward, when the pain began to go out of his body, when his pulpy, battered face had begun to heal.

The day had begun much the same as any day did. It differed in that, after breakfast was finished, Dan's father asked him to ride up to John Mallory's Ox-Yoke and check Mallory's head gate. The man was an incorrigible water thief.

Herb Iles, Dan's father, had the first water right on Crooked Creek, but right now he wasn't getting enough water to irrigate his hayfields, let alone the oats that were just beginning to head. Herb wanted Dan to see how much water Mallory was using. He was careful to caution: "Mind now, if he's taking too much, you ain't to say nothing to him. Just come back here and tell me. I'll handle John Mallory."

Dan saddled up and rode away immediately. Dan was a tall youngster, just turned eighteen. He was stringy from growth, and his shoulders were just beginning to broaden. Dark-haired, dark-eyed, he slumped loosely in the saddle as he rode. The warm spring air was fragrant and pleasant in his nostrils, the sun hot on his back. Overhead, a flock of ravens wheeled and harshly screamed.

Cattle spotted the gray expanse of sagebrush that lay between the two ranches — dark red, sleek, and filling out from new green feed. Here and there newborn calves tottered on wobbly legs, and occasionally one would scamper from Dan's path in mock terror, tail held high like a banner.

A morning to make a man feel the goodness of living, and Dan was feeling it. No foreboding oppressed him; no uneasiness stirred in his mind.

At nine, when Dan reached the Ox-Yoke head gate, it was wide open, as he had expected it would be. Below it, the creek was almost dry. All the water that should have been coming on to the ILS was going into the Ox-Yoke's ditch. Dan felt an instant stir of anger, and a compulsion to close the Ox-Yoke head gate.

In time, however, he remembered his father's admonition and, shrugging regretfully, reined his horse around to start for home. Only this time, instead of cutting through the sagebrush on the south side of Crooked Creek, he took the road that was quicker.

On his right lay the newly green fields of the Ox-Yoke. The ditches that ran above and through them brimmed with glistening water — ILS water. Ahead lay the Ox-Yoke buildings, scattered haphazardly over five acres of bare ground.

The yard was deserted. The corral was empty. Dan hesitated for a moment at the Ox-Yoke gate, still feeling the compulsion to jump Mallory about stealing the water. He was about to ride on when he saw Mrs. Mallory, waving to him from the porch.

She was a pretty woman, as could be seen even at this distance, and she was smiling. Although Dan had not spoken to her over half a dozen times, he was susceptible at eighteen and had felt her attraction before. Her wave became a summons as he started to turn away, so, flushing slightly, he reined in at the gate and rode toward the house.

Susan Mallory was not only pretty; she was undeniably beautiful. Only three years older than Dan himself, she was tall and full-bodied, sparkling-eyed and smiling. Friendly. Perhaps, too friendly.

Dan sat his old saddle, looking down at

173

her. He wished he did not feel so warm. That damned sun! He thumbed back his hat and wiped sweat from his forehead with the back of his hand.

This seemed to give Susan her cue. "Hot, Dan? How about a glass of cold milk and a piece of cherry pie?"

He wanted to refuse, but he hated to be unsociable. He said: "Well, sure, I guess so. I reckon that'd be fine." He dismounted and stepped up onto the porch.

Susan didn't move, and, when Dan reached the top step, he found himself only short inches away from her. He flushed, and Susan laughed, a low, throaty laugh that made Dan flush even more furiously. He hated himself for his embarrassment. He felt that she was laughing at him, yet there was no ridicule in her glance. Rather an invitation, a suggestion. She put up a hand and touched his cheek.

"Dan, you're sweet."

For an instant she stared up into his eyes. Dan felt something entirely new stirring in him. He had kissed girls before, yet this was different, more compelling. Abruptly Susan turned and led the way into the kitchen. Dan took off his hat and stood at the door, turning it around nervously in his hands.

Susan, her nearness, her pleasant intimacy, made the blood pound in his veins. And suddenly Dan knew he ought to go. Susan Mallory was John Mallory's wife, and it wasn't right to think of her the way Dan Iles was thinking of her.

But Dan didn't go. Susan poured out a glass of milk and set it in the center of the table. Dan hesitated, opened his mouth to begin his excuses. Susan paused before him on her way to the cupboard for a plate. Her eyes were wide, excited, her lips slightly parted and moist. The light fragrance of her rose in heady waves to Dan's nostrils. He could feel a light trembling of expectancy as it started in his body.

Then suddenly, terrifyingly so, Susan was close beside him, her arms reaching up behind his neck, pulling his head down toward hers. Dan was scared, more scared than he had ever been in his life before. He reached up and back, seizing her wrists, seeking to pull her arms from around his neck. Her body was hot, tight against him. She was murmuring soft, indistinguishable words. The panic in Dan grew, even in the face of a new and growing desire. And then the door opened behind Dan.

Frantically he yanked Susan's arms down, pushed her away from him. He whirled, knowing with sick dread what he would see.

John Mallory. Big John Mallory. The Ox-Yoke rancher towered an inch above Dan, and outweighed him by sixty pounds. He was tough, all hard bone and muscle. Fifty years old he was, seamed and leathery of face, hard and callused of hand.

How could a man explain another man's wife in his arms? How explain when the husband's eyes were like those of a maddened bull, when his face was suffused with pounding blood, when his lips were quivering with insane fury?

Mallory roared: "So he's the one? Why, damn you!"

One of his big fists banged like a ten-pound sledge on the side of Dan Iles's head. Stunned, his head ringing, Dan flew half across the room, sprawled on the floor. Susan uttered one shrill scream, then scurried across the room to cower against the far wall.

Dan struggled to his knees. He was half blind, groggy, but he made it to his feet before Mallory's fist exploded against his mouth. His lips split against his teeth. He tasted blood, and spat it out. He got up again and staggered toward Mallory. Rage was churning in Dan's brain, but he knew he was helpless before Mallory's crazed power.

Again and again and again, Mallory's fists

crashed into his face. When he began to weaken too much, Mallory switched his attack, concentrating on painful but not incapacitating body punches.

An eternity began for Dan, getting up, being smashed down, getting up again. Each time he was a little slower, but he would not give up. Dimmer and dimmer to his brain came Mallory's panting, savage curses, dimmer the soft cries of protest and sympathy from Susan Mallory's lips.

The time came, as he had known it would, when he could no longer get up, yet he did not wholly lose consciousness. He could hear Mallory cursing his wife, could hear her sobbing.

After a long time, he felt Mallory's hands on him. He was dragged out the door. Mallory made Susan lead his horse close to the porch, and pitched him up into his saddle. A dipperful of water squarely in Dan's face roused him enough for him to hang onto the saddle horn. Then he started his long ride home.

Each step the horse took jarred him. A dozen times he swayed and nearly fell from the saddle. His eyes began to swell, and after a while he could see only with difficulty through narrow slits. His lips puffed, and his body ached with every tiny movement.

Enormous anger began to grow in him, but eventually even this died before the mists that drifted across his mind.

He had no recollection at all of the last two miles before he reached home, nor of his father lifting him down, carrying him in the house, nor of the cold cloths with which his shocked and raging father bathed the blood from his face.

For three days, Herb Iles stayed by his son's side, leaving only for short periods to attend to necessary chores. He ignored his irrigating. He had nothing at all to go on, for Dan lay in a semi-coma all that time, unspeaking, apparently not even thinking. Most of the time Dan slept. What muttering he did in his sleep was incomprehensible to Herb, even though he leaned close to listen.

Herb waited, while slow and terrible anger burned and grew in his heart. So far as Herb was concerned, only one man could have so beaten Dan. Only one man — John Mallory. But why? For God's sake, why? Surely Mallory wouldn't beat a boy like that in a wrangle over water. What, then, could have caused such terrible rage in Mallory? Whatever it was, Herb swore a silent oath that Dan would be avenged.

On the fourth day, Dan's eyes were clear. His face was still scarcely recognizable, but his eyes were clear. Sitting up in his bed, he licked his swollen lips and said: "How'd I get here?"

His father crossed the room at once from the stove where he had been kindling a fire. The air, drifting in the open door, was sharp and fresh, carrying with it the smell of green, growing things, of sage, of dust, and corral manure.

Herb Iles said: "You rode here. Can you tell me what happened now?"

Dan frowned, grimaced at the pain of the frown, then swung his legs over the side of the bunk. He winced as he did, then felt gingerly of his ribs.

Herb said: "None of them broken. What happened?"

"I got whipped. My God, I got whipped."

Into Dan's mind now flooded all the things that had happened, bitter, shameful memories. He had not been at fault, but who would believe that? And he had suffered more at Mallory's hands than any man should. He was deeply ashamed, deeply humiliated.

"Who did it?" His father was growing irritated, angry.

"Mallory."

"Why? Why? Not over that water, surely. I told you. . . ."

Dan stood up experimentally. "No. It wasn't about water. It was about. . . ." He hesitated, finally said: "It was about Mallory's wife."

His father stared at him, stunned. "You and her . . . ?"

Dan shook his head. "Mallory was wrong." He sat back down and dropped his head into his hands. His voice was low, bitter. "I went up and looked at the head gate. Mallory was taking all the water, just like we figured. I came back by way of the road, and, as I passed their gate, I saw her beckoning to me. Well, I rode in. Who wouldn't?"

"What happened then?"

"She was kind of acting funny. Friendly. It embarrassed me." Dan could feel his face flushing, remembering this. "She offered me a glass of milk and a piece of pie. I didn't want it, but I didn't know how to say no. I got down and went in the kitchen. Next thing I knew, she had her arms around my neck. And about that time, in comes John Mallory." He scowled. Telling it, even knowing it was true, it had a fishy sound. He said stubbornly: "Mallory didn't give me time to open my mouth. He slammed me on the side of the head and knocked me half across the room." His voice assumed a somber bitterness, "I never got set. Every time I'd get up, he'd be there, and he'd hit me again. After a while, all I could do was get up, and pretty soon after that I couldn't even get up."

Herb Iles grunted. "That's all I wanted to know."

He got up and settled his hat on his head. From a nail on the wall he took down his holstered Colt .44 and cartridge belt, something he rarely wore.

Dan said: "No! Wait a minute. This ain't your battle. I'll get square with Mallory myself."

"No. I'll get square with him. If you was even close to his size, I'd not say a word. But, by hell, he's too damned big for you, and he ain't for me."

He whirled and strode out of the door, ignoring Dan's shouted plea for him to stop. Dan grabbed for his pants, but before he got them on, he heard the drum of hoofs in the lane.

His father had gone.

Chapter Two

Dan Iles ached in every muscle. Bending over to put on his boots was torture. But he forgot all that in the desperate urgency of the moment. He got the boots on and slipped into a clean shirt. Looking around for a gun, he found a rifle leaning in one corner. There was a box of cartridges in a cupboard above it, and he dumped half the box into his pants pocket.

When he went outside, weakness and dizziness made his head reel. Fortunately there was a horse in the corral. Dan roped the horse, a dappled gray, and threw his old saddle up onto its back. As he mounted and spurred savagely out of the yard, he could see his father a full three miles away now, merely a dark speck on the road.

The gray took the turn from lane to road at a hard run. To a well man, it would have seemed a flowing, easy gait. To Dan it seemed a bone-breaking one. He felt a mild amazement that Mallory could have inflicted such punishment upon him.

He thought of Susan Mallory, and a seed of anger was planted in his mind. *Damn her! Damn them both!* Dan had been guilty of nothing, and he knew he never would have laid a hand on Susan Mallory. She had thrown herself into his arms. And he had paid the penalty.

Yet, for some reason, Dan found himself blaming not Susan, but her husband. Mallory had been too quick to accuse, too quick to exact vengeance. If Susan hated her husband, if she sought consolation with other men, Dan was damned if he could find it in his heart to blame her. He hated Mallory himself. Hated him with a consuming, overpowering intensity. He wondered what his father had in mind, what he intended to do when he reached Mallory's Ox-Yoke. His father's words had indicated he intended to whip Mallory with his fists. Yet he had belted on his gun.

Dan spurred his horse, urged him to an even greater speed. The gray reached out eagerly, and Dan gritted his teeth against the pain in his bruised and beaten body.

He wished he could down the heavy, cold feeling of uneasiness that created a core of ice in his stomach. It was foreboding; it was prescient terror. His horse was giving his utmost, but Dan knew suddenly it would not be enough. By the time he reached the Ox-Yoke, it would be all over.

He could not have said how he knew. But he did. Herb Iles and John Mallory would not fight with their fists. They would fight with their guns.

Why was Dan so sure that Herb would be the loser? He shook his head impatiently, telling himself: *You don't know. You couldn't.* But there was no conviction in him. No conviction and no hope.

As Herb Iles rode, he let the anger grow within him unchecked, knowing that he was being foolishly reckless. Yet for three days he had sat by his son's side, watching Dan's torment, his pain. He had heard Dan's tormented muttering. Herb Iles had seen many men who had been badly beaten, but he doubted if he had ever seen anyone hurt quite as badly as Dan had been. And all for nothing. It was that damned woman who had deserved the beating.

Herb Iles didn't know Susan Mallory well. Like Dan, he'd not spoken to her over half a dozen times. But he knew her type. He had long ago sensed her faithlessness, that one man could never be enough for her. And he knew Mallory. Mallory was the kind in whom jealousy is corrosive. Herb thought he knew about what had happened to lead up to Dan's beating.

Mallory, away from home considerably as most cowmen were, had perhaps for a long time suspected that all was not right in his home. Maybe he'd found small bits of evidence upon his return a time or two. At any rate, on the day of Dan's beating, he'd only pretended to leave. He'd hidden somewhere on the premises, to watch and wait. Dan, beckoned in from the gate, had come, as anyone would have done. In this country, when a woman beckoned a man in from the road, it usually meant she needed help of some sort. And Dan had not ignored her plea.

Dan was a handsome kid, his father thought, and not much younger than Susan. He could understand how a woman would find Dan attractive. Herb flushed briefly with anger. Dan was like all kids of that age, putty in the hands of a clever, wanton woman. Probably there would have been no more than a kiss between them. Probably Dan would have shied off and run before it came to more than that. But Mallory had jumped to the conclusion that Dan was his wife's lover. Dan had taken the beating for someone else.

Well, after today, John Mallory would

make more certain before he piled into an innocent kid. Herb Iles's jaw hardened with determination. Herb was as tall as Dan, but he was a lot more solid, and he was not yet forty. He was as tough as latigo leather, lighter than John Mallory, perhaps, but younger, and stronger. He'd give Mallory the twin of the beating Mallory had handed Dan. The thought gave Herb such pleasure he grinned wolfishly.

He pushed his horse hard, for he was anxious for this to begin. The miles flowed beneath the animal's pounding hoofs, and at last Herb came to the Ox-Yoke gate. He could see the fields from here, could see the overflow of water from the ditches into the fields. That was another score he had to settle with Mallory. He shrugged, grinning slightly. Just as well add water theft to his reasons for whipping Mallory. Just as well land a few extra solid punches for the water.

Mallory was home. Herb could tell that, because Mallory's horse was tied to a tree near the kitchen door. An irrigating shovel leaned against the wall of the house with fresh mud still clinging to it. Out in the corral were perhaps a dozen cows, their unbranded calves by their sides. A fire, just kindled, was burning inside the corral.

Mallory had been irrigating earlier this

186

morning. A few minutes before, he had been getting ready to brand a few slick calves. But he had left his branding fire at Herb Iles's approach. He would be watching, now, from the house.

An odd tingle of uneasiness ran along Herb's spine. It wasn't like Mallory to scoot for the house. It wasn't like him to hide. Whatever he was, he was not a coward. Why, then, was he hiding? Why was he not here in the yard, ready to face whatever he had coming?

Herb's uneasiness increased. He had that odd feeling that comes to a man when he is being watched. He tried to spot Mallory, staring at first one window and then another, but all were heavily curtained, although probably Mallory was watching him from behind the curtains.

He swung down from his horse and, dropping the reins, approached the house. He lifted his voice in a hoarse shout: "Mallory! Damn you, come out of there! I've come to settle for that beating you gave Dan!"

He caught a stir of movement at one of the windows, saw the curtain thrust aside. He heard the tinkle of breaking glass. He could not miss the long, blued muzzle of a rifle that poked out at him.

He yelled: "Mallory, don't be a fool! It's

fists I've got in mind!"

The rifle muzzle steadied on him. In sudden panic, Herb Iles dived aside. The rifle muzzle followed him. That was all he could see, just the rifle's gaping muzzle.

He had thought it a threat at first. Suddenly he knew that it was not a threat at all. John Mallory intended to kill him. His hand flew to the holstered gun at his side, clumsily, for Herb Iles was no gunfighter. And smoke belched from the rifle's muzzle in the window.

Herb Iles's Colt thudded into the dust at his side. He jerked convulsively. He stared at the rifle in the window, at the light plume of smoke curling up from it, with utter amazement on his face. He took three hesitant steps toward the house, then he folded quietly forward onto the ground, and lay still. Inside the house a woman began to scream imprecations. This continued uninterrupted for perhaps a minute. Then there was the sound of something thrown, and the woman's voice was silent.

A man's voice, a heavy voice, began to curse. The rifle bore steadily on Herb Iles's still body, and did not pull back until the hoofbeats of Dan's horse sounded in the lane.

Chapter Three

Before Dan Iles reached the Ox-Yoke gate, he had heard the shot. He turned in through the gate without slacking pace, and thundered down toward the Mallory house. He could see his father's body, still on the ground before the house. And that was all he could see. No one was in the yard with his father.

Wild terror and crazy rage tore at Dan, leaving only one thing clear. His father had been shot from ambush, from a window in the house! He'd never had a chance!

Dan had to get to his father immediately. He was two hundred yards from the house when awareness of how stupid that would be struck him with all its force. He yanked back on the reins savagely. The gray plunged to a stop, and Dan hit the ground, running. He let the momentum of the horse's forward movement carry him to an angle across the lane and into the brushy tangle along the fence. He dived into that brush and flung himself to the ground an instant before a bullet sang over his head.

For a moment he lay still, panting, scared. He'd never been fired at before. Then he thought of his father, so still in the yard, maybe needing help, maybe only unconscious and not dead.

He had clung to the rifle as he came off his horse. Now he suddenly realized that it was in his hand. He fished in his pants pocket for shells and loaded the gun with trembling fingers. Another shot probed the brush for him, clipping a couple of twigs that dropped onto the back of his neck. Instinctively he ducked.

With the gun loaded, he shoved it out before him and began to crawl — carefully so as not to stir the tips of the brush and give his movement away. As he came to a spot from which he could see the house, he saw that the sun was shining on the windows in such a way that he immediately spotted the broken one. And he saw the rifle muzzle poking out. Carefully lining his sights, he squeezed the trigger.

His bullet smacked into something solid. The rifle muzzle in the window disappeared as if by magic. Dan levered the rifle and put a second shot after the first. Then he waited.

For an instant there was utter silence. Then he heard Susan Mallory scream. The kitchen door burst open, and she came running out. Her hands went to her mouth when she saw Herb Iles, and she screamed again.

Halted, she stared wildly around, calling: "Dan! Dan! Don't shoot me!"

Dan raised his head. His harsh voice was certainly not the voice of an eighteen-year-old. "Where's Mallory?"

"You hit him! Oh Dan! Dan!"

Dan got up and ran toward the house, expecting trickery, expecting Mallory's shot to take him any instant. Susan was clutching at him, but he threw her aside so roughly that she sprawled on the ground. She didn't get up.

Dan's glance touched Herb's still figure. He wanted to stop, wanted to terribly, but knew he could not. He burst into the house on a dead run and was halfway across the kitchen before he could stop.

The room stirred memories of horror in him, memories of that terrible beating. Mallory was on the floor, but Mallory was not dead. Dan centered the rifle on Mallory's head, between the eyes. And as suddenly he lowered it. He couldn't kill a man like he would a dog, an unconscious man. Not even if that man had killed Herb.

Beside Mallory lay the shattered rifle with which the big rancher had shot Herb. Its stock was splintered from Dan's bullet, which apparently had struck the rifle and glanced off, striking Mallory. There was a long, nasty ragged gash in the side of Mallory's head from which blood oozed freely.

Dan wheeled and went outside. Mallory wouldn't be coming to for a while. Dan knelt beside his father, turned him gently onto his back. He dropped his head to Herb's chest, listening intently. He heard nothing, nothing at all. He grabbed Herb by his shoulders and shook him. He could feel hysteria rising within him.

Susan's soft voice came from behind him. "Dan . . . Dan, I'm so sorry. I'm so terribly sorry."

His eyes were wild as he turned, and his voice broke: "Shut up! Let me alone! Let me alone!"

Herb's horse had wandered across the yard to the corral. Dan got up and went over to him, led him back. The tension in Dan Iles was intolerable. He hadn't cried for years, but he could feel tears starting in his eyes now — tears of grief, of rage, of frustration.

He tried to lift his father's body to the horse's back, but the animal kept shying away, and the body was too heavy for him.

Susan moved close to help, and Dan tolerated this, knowing he must.

They got Herb on the horse's back, and Dan tied him down with a lariat. He picked up Herb's gun and shoved it into his belt.

Susan was utterly silent, and he didn't look at her. He ran across the yard and caught his own horse, led him back to where Herb's horse stood.

Susan was still silent, and Dan shot a glance at her. She stood with her head slightly bent, with her hands outspread and upturned before her. She was staring at a thick red stain on her hands, at Herb Iles's blood.

Dan mounted. Susan began to weep hysterically. She began to wipe her hands on her dress. She was still wiping her blood-stained hands as Dan rode away — as though no amount of wiping could take the stain away. And perhaps it couldn't.

Although he did not realize it, Dan Iles was in a serious state of shock. He rode slowly, his head drooping. His eyes were blank, still. He saw nothing, not the road or the landscape, not his horse's head before him. He did not feel the pain in his body now. The pain in his mind obscured it. But the effect of the beating Mallory had given him remained, and, coupled with the shock of Herb's death, it stood a good chance of unseating his reason.

He was unaware of the time it took him to reach home. He turned in through the gate automatically. Moving like a sleepwalker, he dismounted before the house, untied Herb's body, and eased it off into his arms. Staggering under Herb's weight, he walked to the house, up the steps to the porch.

He fumbled helplessly, at the door, and almost dropped his father's body. But he got the door open and went inside. He laid Herb on the bed and stood staring down at him. There was wonder in his eyes, wonder at the speed with which the flame of life could be snuffed out. A part of his mind still refused to accept the fact of death, and he unbuttoned his father's shirt and dropped his head again to Herb's chest. The hole there was blue and round and not big. When Dan stood up, his chin was trembling.

What now? What should he do now? It must be night. So much had happened. But a glance outside told him it was barely noon. He thought of Mallory, and knew he should have killed the man when he had the chance. He owed that much to Herb. And yet he knew that, given the same chance again, his decision would be the same. It was not in him to murder an unconscious man, no matter what that man had done. He felt sure Herb would have approved. His father had been that kind of a man.

Dan felt tears smarting behind his eyes. He thought of town, thought of the sheriff. And without further consideration, he went outside.

He turned Herb's horse into the corral and unsaddled him. Then, mounting his own dappled gray, he set out for town. Herb's gun was still in his belt. Thinking of what he would tell the sheriff, he withdrew it and smelled the barrel. It had not been fired. He checked the chambers, found them all full, except for the one under the hammer.

The gun was evidence enough of murder. The gun and the broken window at the Ox-Yoke. And Susan Mallory's testimony. And Dan's own story. Yes. Mallory would pay the penalty for Herb Iles's murder. There could be no doubt of that.

It was mid-afternoon when Dan rode into Sundance. The town was quiet, drowsing under the hot sun. From the schoolhouse came the drone of a reciting child's voice. A dog sniffed at the heels of Dan's horse incuriously.

The sheriff's office and town jail were squeezed tightly between the courthouse and the Wells Fargo freight dépôt, and beyond that corrals filled with feeding horses occupied almost half a block. Dan dismounted and tied his horse to the rail. A woman in a bright gingham dress looked at him as she passed. Startled at his appearance, her eyes widened and she gave a little gasp. Then her lips tightened with disapproval, and she hurried on.

Dan went into the office. Sheriff Frank Tate, oldish and heavily mustached, looked up, unmoved. When he saw Dan's face, his booted feet came off the desk and hit the floor with a thump. His swivel chair squeaked loudly.

"Good glory, Dan, what happened to you?"

Dan could feel hysteria rising again. He waited a moment before speaking, gaining control of himself. He didn't want to let down, to bawl like a damned baby. He was a man now. He said: "Can I sit down?" His knees were shaking, and he didn't want the sheriff to see that.

"Sure, boy, sure. Sit down. What's the matter? What's happened?"

"Mallory killed Herb . . . murdered him. He shot him out of the window up at the Ox-Yoke."

Tate leaned forward, his face shocked.

But his voice was low, calm. "Why'd he do that, Dan?"

Dan's whole body was shaking. "Mallory worked me over two, three days ago. He thought I was. . . ." Dan gritted his teeth and went on. "He thought I was carrying on with his wife."

"Was you, Dan?"

"No! 'Course, I wasn't." He clasped his hands tightly together on his knees. "Herb went up to kick hell out of him. I tried to stop Herb, and I followed soon as I could. I didn't want Herb fighting my fights for me."

"Sure not." Tate's voice was sympathetic.

"Then Mallory poked a rifle through the window and shot Herb. He was dead when I got there. Mallory began shooting at me. I shot back a couple of times and busted his rifle and nicked his head. I loaded Herb's body on his horse and took him home. Then I came here."

"Mallory ain't dead? You sure?"

"No. He ain't dead. I tried to shoot him when I got in the house, but I couldn't."

Tate got up and reached for his hat. Dan clenched his fists. At eighteen he looked like a man and was a man's size. But he wasn't one yet. Not quite. He was trying, though, trying hard.

Tate said soothingly: "Dan, go on over

there and lay down on that sofa. Get some sleep. I'll lock the office door, so's nobody'll bother you. And I'll go get Mallory."

Dan protested: "I could go with you."

But Tate shook his head. "Uhn-uh. You've stood about enough for one day. You get yourself some sleep. I'll be back with Mallory before nightfall. Then we'll see."

Dan shrugged. He didn't have the strength to protest. Weariness suddenly weighted all his muscles, and the pain of the bruises came back. He said — "All right, Sheriff." — and sat still in the chair while Tate buckled on his guns and belt. The sheriff closed the door behind him, and Dan heard the key turn in the lock.

For an instant it occurred to him that the sheriff might well be locking him in more than locking intruders out. But then he looked at the windows, unbarred, easily opened from the inside. No, he could get out any time he chose. He went over and lay down on the leather-covered sofa. He closed his eyes. After a while, he went to sleep.

Chapter Four

All through the long afternoon, Dan Iles lay tossing on the sheriff's sofa. Semi-conscious, he was tortured by dreams, dreams of death and violence. Twice he awoke, sweating profusely but cold nevertheless.

Dark came, but he did not get up. Exhaustion had taken too heavy a toll. At last, an hour or so after full dark, he heard the key in the door lock.

Nervous instinctively, he sat up, looking around for cover. Then he relaxed. The sheriff came in alone and struck a match. Dan watched silently as Tate touched the match to a lamp wick and lowered the lamp chimney over it. Tate turned to face him then.

Dan said: "Where's Mallory?"

"I didn't bring him in."

"Why not?" Dan's voice rose. "Why didn't you?"

"Dan, take it easy. Mallory says Herb came roaring up to the ranch house, waving his six-shooter, hollering he was going to kill him. Mallory shot him in self-defense, kid."

Stunned, Dan was silent. When he spoke, his voice was soft and low, but deadly. "He's a damned liar, Sheriff."

"His wife backs him up. She says that's just the way it happened."

"Then she's a liar, too."

The sheriff cleared his throat. He would not meet Dan's eyes. He said: "You're sore, kid. You got caught fooling around with Susan, and you got worked over. I ain't saying that Mallory wasn't too damned rough on you. Susan's older'n you, and probably she was more to blame than you was. But you can't blame a man for protecting his home."

Dan's stomach was hollow, empty. He said: "I wasn't fooling around with her."

He told Tate with quick words exactly what had happened the morning Mallory had worked him over. When he finished, Tate was grinning.

"Now, Dan, I can't say I blame a kid for sowing some wild oats. And Susan likely encouraged you plenty. But don't try to make me believe that story, kid. It's too damned thin. Nobody'd believe it, least of all me."

Dan tensed, gathered his legs like springs under him. Raw, uncontrolled anger launched him across the room at the sheriff. His weight and the impact of his body toppled the law man's swivel chair backward. Dan's hands closed over the sheriff's throat.

Tate was a powerful man, heavily muscled from his years in the saddle. But he was no match for the maniacal rage in Dan Iles. Too many things had piled up on Dan, injustice after injustice, until he was almost insane with resentment.

Tate's refusal to arrest Mallory, Dan could have understood, for if Susan backed Mallory's story, there was little else the sheriff could do. But Tate's leering belief that Dan had been Susan Mallory's lover was too much to bear.

Tate was gasping, his face turning blue by the time sanity returned to Dan Iles. Abruptly Dan released him, and the sheriff rolled and began to cough. Dan got up. His hand went to his belt, missed Herb's gun. He searched quickly, retrieved the gun from the floor, and stuffed it back down inside his belt.

The sheriff was sitting up, retching. His eyes glared balefully at Dan, filled with threat and rage.

Dan stalked out of the office and slammed the door behind him. He mounted, and touched the gray with his spurs. Seething, he went out of town at a hard run.

As soon as Dan had left that morning, Susan Mallory had run to the pump. She worked the handle frantically, and filled the bucket that stood under the spout.

She found a small piece of strong laundry soap and lathered her hands furiously. She rinsed them off, and lathered again. Four times she washed her hands, then drying them on her skirt, she went toward the house.

John Mallory was stirring, moaning softly. Susan got a dipperful of water from the table and threw it into his face. She found a clean towel and, controlling her nausea with difficulty, bathed the bullet gash on the side of his head.

Apparently the bullet had split up the rifle butt, and one of the fragments had torn this gash, for it was ragged, the flesh in shreds. But it obviously was not serious.

The pain of her ministrations roused Mallory, and he struggled to sit up. Susan pushed him back down on the floor, saying: "Lie still till I finish, John."

From another clean towel she tore strips and bandaged his head. The flow of blood had almost stopped now. Mallory kept shutting his eyes, kept wrinkling his forehead, and Susan knew he had a splitting, terrible headache. And no wonder. He was lucky he wasn't dead.

She helped him to his feet, helped him out of the kitchen, and into the neat parlor. She helped him sit in an upholstered rocker.

Mallory said: "What happened?"

"You killed Herb Iles. Dan came riding in, and you shot at him. Dan shot back. One of his bullets struck your rifle and glanced off. You've got a bad gash in your head, but that's all. You're lucky."

He dropped his forehead into his hands and groaned. Susan's voice became contemptuous. "The sheriff will be here soon. You'll be wanted for murder. You never gave Herb Iles a chance."

His head came up. His eyes, bloodshot and staring, glared at her. "If you weren't such a. . . ."

"With that boy?" She laughed harshly. "He was half scared to death when you walked in. He was trying to get away from me." Her expression softened a little, and she licked her lips. "If I'd had a little more time, though. . . ."

Mallory came out of his chair. Rage bubbled out of his mouth like a groan. His hands were spread, reaching for her. She evaded him easily, and laughed again.

"Don't put your hands on me, John Mallory. You're forgetting something, aren't you? I'm the only person alive who can keep a rope from around your neck. Suppose I should tell the sheriff the truth about what happened here today?"

The rage drained out of Mallory like water being poured out of a pail. He stopped, swaying in the center of the room. "Susan, don't do that."

"Why not? I'm sick of you! I'm sick of living in this damned shack, away out in the wilderness. I'm sick of your damned stinginess."

"I'll give you some money, Susan. I'll give you enough for a new dress. I'll drive you to town this afternoon, so's you can get it."

Susan stared at him. Her eyes were wide with a sudden realization. Mallory would do what she wanted him to do, now.

She crossed the room and sank into a chair. A whole new vista of promise opened up before her. No more living in this sagging log house. No more doing without pretty clothes, good times. She could go to Denver, and Mallory would send her money. She'd make him send her money. He couldn't refuse, because, if he did, Susan would tell the sheriff the truth.

She said: "John, I'm going to Denver to-morrow. I'm going to stay there for a while. All this trouble has been too much for me. I think I can get along on about five hundred dollars to start with." She was smiling oddly.

Shudders ran through John Mallory. For a long while he stared at her as though he could not believe what he saw. When he nodded, it was almost as though he were in a daze. "All right, Sue. You'll get your money."

Susan got up. "Now that's settled, you lie down. You'll need your strength when you talk to the sheriff. Tell him that Herb Iles came riding in here, brandishing his gun, threatening to kill you. You shot him in self-defense. Tell the sheriff that Dan and I were carrying on behind your back." She smiled. "I won't deny it. I'll blush and look ashamed, and the sheriff will believe that, too."

Mallory's big fists kept clenching and un-clenching. He kept his eyes on the floor be-tween his feet. Susan thought: *Just as well give it all to him right now.* Aloud she said: "Oh, John . . . one more thing. I don't sup-pose that five hundred will last too long. So you get busy and think of some way to get more, won't you?"

For what seemed an eternity to her,

Mallory's body was wholly stiff. His hands stopped their nervous clenching and un-clenching. He scarcely seemed to breathe. But at last he nodded wearily. "All right, Sue. All right."

Sue's expression was sober. She touched his gray hair with her hand. "Now you lie down and rest until the sheriff comes."

"All right, Sue."

He got up and crossed the room to the sofa, sank down onto it with a grateful sigh. Susan smiled with satisfaction that was al-most feline and tiptoed from the room, closing the door behind her.

John Mallory closed his eyes, lying utterly still. He could hear Susan moving around as she began to pack her valise. She began to hum softly.

He could not have said now exactly why he had fired at Herb from the window. He was not a coward, at least had never consid-ered himself one. Perhaps his reluctance to face Herb, to take Herb's beating, had stemmed from a sneaking suspicion that he had been wrong about Dan and Susan. That morning he had been insane with jealous rage. He had not looked at things objec-tively. He had only been conscious of Susan in Dan's arms, and the pain of seeing that had nearly driven him mad. Also, for some time now he had known Susan was having visitors whenever he was away from home. He had found horse tracks overlying his own half a dozen times. He had noticed a difference in Susan on each of those occasions.

Well, he conceded, a man was a fool to marry a woman so much younger than him, no matter how virile he was. He was only courting trouble when he did. *Let her go.* His face twisted, and his mouth turned ugly. *Let her go!* He laughed harshly, aloud. *If thy hand offend thee, cut it off!* He laughed again. Words. How could he stand to be without her? How could he tolerate the deadly silence of the night alone? How could he assuage the aching longing that would torment him, the longing to hold her in his arms?

Restlessly, nervously, he got up and began to pace the floor. And how could he keep her supplied with money? The Ox-Yoke was a good ranch. Given more water, it would be a better one. Mallory had a hundred acres in hay now. If he had plenty of water, he could put another five hundred acres in hay and grain. He could double, triple the carrying capacity of the ranch. And with more land under the ditch, there wasn't a bank in the territory that would refuse him money to buy more cattle.

Water. Water. That was the rub, the stumbling block. But if he had water. . . . His mind began to explore the possibilities. He began to visualize what the Ox-Yoke could be. The ranch could carry a thousand head of cattle instead of the measly two hundred it was carrying now. He could build a big house, a new house, here, for Susan. He could bring in furniture she would like, could buy her all the new clothes she wanted. He could take her on trips to Denver, Cheyenne, perhaps even San Francisco. He could hold her, keep her.

But first he had to have water. And there was only one place he could get it. From the Ileses.

He stopped at the window and stared out into the yard. He could see the corral, could see the handful of cows he had run in there earlier today along with their blatting calves. He ought to get out there and put his brand on them, so he could turn them out. He hated to think of having to gather them again. He hated to turn them out unbranded. But his head ached — ached terribly. He put his hands up and rubbed his forehead, squinting.

Suddenly he straightened. For a long moment he stared at the corral, at the dark red shapes behind the pole fence. His eyes widened with some sudden realization. And at last he began to grin.

There was a way out of this, after all. Quietly he made his way out through the door. He crossed the yard, gathered up an armload of wood, and went to the corral. He built his fire swiftly, expertly, putting his branding irons in the fire. He got a lariat down from the corral fence and roped one of the calves.

He threw it, hogtied it. Then he went back to watch his irons. When they were hot, he pulled one out of the fire and went to the calf. He began to brand, but it was not Ox-Yoke he put on the calf's hip. It was ILS. And it was the Iles earmark he used on the calf's ears. Swiftly he put the ILS brand on a second calf. Then he opened the gate and turned the bunch out. He watched them, as they headed for the creek, crossed it, and began to climb through the high sagebrush onto the hillside. Now all John Mallory had to do was wait.

Someday, soon now, he'd hire a man in Sundance to help with the spring branding. During the course of the work, they were sure to run upon the two calves, branded ILS but running with Ox-Yoke cows. Mallory would send his man after the sheriff. He began to chuckle. It was ridiculously simple, ridiculously sure. He could even imagine the sheriff's words, spoken in his judicious, measured voice. "Hell, Mallory, the kid was sore. You whipped him for messing with your wife. Then you had to kill his pa. He figured to get even like any kid might. But being a kid, he wasn't too smart about it. He figured he'd run his brand on a few of your calves, then push them on the cows somewhere where they wouldn't be seen until next winter when he'd wean the calves. But a couple of 'em strayed back, and now I reckon we've got the goods on Dan."

Smiling enigmatically, Mallory slipped quietly back into the house. Susan, apparently preoccupied with her packing and her planning, was still humming to herself in the bedroom. Mallory lay back down on the sofa and closed his eyes. He was sure Susan had not seen him leave. He was sure that his branding had gone unobserved.

His head still ached, but that couldn't kill his pleasure now. Smiling, his mind teeming with plans, he relaxed to wait for the sheriff.

Chapter Five

Not one thing did Dan Iles know about the formalities and the mechanics of a burial. What he did know was that he couldn't face the people of the town, knowing they believed him guilty of carrying on with Susan Mallory, knowing they believed his father guilty of an armed attack on Mallory himself. All that night he sat in a chair at home, staring out the window. He found it unbelievable that so much trouble had stemmed from such a simple thing as his responding to Susan Mallory's beckoning wave.

To Dan's mind, the terrible part of it was that neither Herb nor he had done anything that could be considered wrong. Yet Herb was dead, and his murderer free, absolved. Dan had taken a terrible beating, which was not in itself as important as the fact that he stood convicted in the minds of the people who knew him, convicted of tampering with the sanctity of Mallory's home.

Well, he'd not bury Herb in town. He'd not let them stand around blaming Herb because his violence had brought about his death. He'd not let them pity Herb because his son had erred, because Herb had not been able to believe it of him. He'd bury him here, where Herb had lived, where the two of them had been so happy for so long a time.

At dawn, he went out and began to build Herb's coffin. By mid-morning he had it finished. He dressed Herb in his broadcloth suit, put a bunch of blankets in the coffin, and laid Herb in. He nailed the lid down with tears streaming down his face. Then he went out beneath the big willow tree and began to dig the grave.

The ground was soft and moist. Occasionally he would strike one of the willow roots and have to cut it off with the axe. But by mid-afternoon he had the grave finished and dragged the coffin to it with a lariat and saddle horse.

He went into the house and got down the big family Bible. His father had not been a religious man. Dan doubted if the book had been opened since his mother's death. But he stood beside the grave and silently read from the Book for nearly thirty minutes before he put it aside.

Something about the reading had calmed his mind. Something of the age-old wisdom in the Book had permeated his thoughts. He rigged a tripod from poles and with block and tackle lowered Herb's casket into the grave. Covering it was the hardest — shoveling the dirt in on top of it. He was white-faced and weak when he finished.

The rest of the day he spent in making a wooden headstone, in carving Herb's name in the wood. When he finally finished, it was growing dark.

Dan realized that he had not eaten for twenty-four hours. He wasn't hungry, but he knew he needed food for strength, so he opened a can of beans and wolfed it down cold. He made a pot of coffee afterward and drank four steaming cups of it.

By then he had regained his composure. His face had become still and calm. He had aged a lot in the last four days. Taking his father's cartridge belt from the bed where he had laid it, he emptied the .44 and seated it in the holster. Then he buckled the whole thing around his middle and began to practice — draw and fire, draw and fire. There was no selfconsciousness in doing this, nor was there any particular pleasure, either. It was as though he thought of it only as something that had to be done. The law had refused to avenge Herb's murder. But the murder would not go unavenged.

Something he had read in the old Bible stuck in his mind. *An eye for an eye, a tooth for a tooth.* And a phrase of his own always followed it: *A life for a life.*

The days marched past in orderly, measured sequence. Dan Iles stayed on the ranch, irrigating with what water Mallory allowed to go past his own head gate. Dan knew he should go up and settle the water question with Mallory, but he couldn't trust himself to talk to the man. And he wasn't yet ready to kill him.

Nights, he practiced with the .44.

At first, he had half expected Frank Tate to press charges against him for the attack he had made on the sheriff in his office the night Herb was killed. Tate never showed up. Dan was grateful for that. But the irony of it didn't escape him. Attacking Tate was the one thing he had done that was wrong. And it was the only thing for which he hadn't paid.

Dan knew when Mallory hired a couple of riders in Sundance, apparently to help with the calf branding, for he saw the three heading toward the Ox-Yoke about a week after Herb's death. Another two days went by and he saw one of Mallory's new hands riding for town one morning. Several hours later, when the man returned, the sheriff was riding beside him.

Uneasiness stirred in Dan Iles. Uneasiness and a strange new fear. What was Mallory up to now? Hadn't he done enough damage?

Not knowing quite why, Dan saddled a horse, the best one he had, a sorrel gelding named Rusty. He filled a sack with beans and coffee, a frying pan, and coffee pot. He tied a blanket roll on behind his saddle with his grub sack, got the rifle, and shoved it into the boot. Rummaging through the house for all the cartridges he could find, he put them in his pockets. He led Rusty behind the house and tied him. Then he settled down to wait.

He didn't have long. No more than ten minutes passed before he saw them coming. Tate. Mallory. The two new Ox-Yoke riders.

They weren't satisfied. They still wanted something from him. Well, by the eternal, he'd give it to them. His hand dropped, caressed the worn walnut grips of the .44. He stood on the porch and waited, tall, thin, still showing the blue of bruises on his face. His eyes were cold and hard. Two weeks ago he had been a boy. Now he was a man grown. He let them ride in, let them group in a semi-circle before him.

Tate asked: "How many of Mallory's calves did you put your ILS on, Dan?"

"Not a damned one."

Tate shook his head, grimly smiling. "It won't do, boy. It won't do. Mallory just got through showing me two fresh-branded ILS calves sucking on Ox-Yoke cows. Where'd you hide the others?"

Dan looked from the sheriff's face to Mallory's. Mallory tried hard to meet his glance, but he couldn't cut it. He looked away. Dan looked at the two riders. Their eyes were cold. To them and to the sheriff he was a rustler. Only Mallory knew the truth. Mallory had rigged this himself. Maybe he'd deliberately branded some of his own calves ILS.

Why? Why was Mallory so determined to ruin Dan? Did he really believe that Dan had been his wife's lover? Dan's shoulders lifted in an imperceptible shrug.

Tate growled: "Git your horse and come along, Dan."

Two weeks ago, Dan would have gone meekly enough. Two weeks ago Dan still had a boy's faith in justice, in the essential fairness of the law. But that was changed now. That was all changed. He had seen too much of injustice since then.

He was old enough, wise enough to know he was close to death. He had no intention of allowing the sheriff to take him. And the only way to avoid that was to fight.

Fight four determined men. He made himself shrug, made his shoulders sag dispiritedly. He half turned away toward the house, saying — "I need a couple of things." — and from the corner of his eye saw them relax.

The sheriff started to dismount on the far side of his horse, the left side. Half in saddle, half out, he said: "No damned tricks, Dan."

Dan's hand snaked downward after the .44. His thumb fumbled the hammer, but it was a good, fast draw anyway. He caught them by surprise. They hadn't expected resistance from him in spite of the gun he wore.

Hating Mallory the way he did, he put his first shot in Mallory's direction. He was flustered and scared. He shot too soon. But the bullet went through the neck of Mallory's horse just as Mallory spurred him off to one side. The horse pitched forward, end over end. Mallory screamed as the saddle horn gouged his leg, and after that he was pinned underneath the horse that didn't move.

Dan's second shot entered the sheriff's horse just behind the shoulder. The animal gave a great, spasmodic leap, throwing the sheriff off balance, leaving him without protection. Mallory's two riders had their hands full with their plunging horses that apparently were unused to gunfire. Both men had guns in their hands, but had no chance to use them.

Dan's shout was ragged and hoarse. "Drop them damned guns!"

Dan's mind was working with lightning speed now. The sheriff's gun was half drawn, but the sheriff was hesitating as Dan's .44 swung to cover him. Dan knew if he had taken the time to fire at Mallory's riders, the sheriff would have finished his draw. Now Dan could fairly see the law man's mind changing.

He said: "Drop it before I kill you!"

The sheriff's hand fell away from the gun grip. The two 'punchers were still doubtful, but when they saw Tate under Dan's steady gun, they let their own guns drop to the ground. Both dismounted from their spooked and plunging horses, looking dismayed.

Mallory kept yelling: "Tate! For God's sake, get this horse off me!"

Dan grunted to Tate: "Leave him be. Turn around, Sheriff."

Tate complied with obvious reluctance, but he complied. He had seen something in Dan Iles's eyes that he didn't particularly like. Wildness. Panic, maybe. Unpredictability. Dan Iles had been pushed as far as he could be pushed. He was as dangerous in this moment as a cornered cougar. And his gun was steady.

Dan walked over and lifted Tate's gun from its holster, then crossed and picked up the two 'punchers' guns. He stuffed all three down inside his belt. Carefully, then, he circled Mallory's downed horse. Mallory grabbed for his ankle, and Dan instantly brought the barrel of the .44 down in a vicious, flashing arc. Mallory slumped limply against the ground. Dan stooped over and got his gun, which was still in its holster.

Bending over, with four guns stuffed in his belt, was something of a chore. But Dan, pocketknife in his left hand, stooped and cut the cinches on Mallory's saddle.

Tate started to protest as Dan cut the sheriff's cinch, but a glance from Dan killed the protest on his lips. Dan cut the cinches on both of the 'punchers' saddles, unbridled the horses, and turned them loose. At a fast trot, they headed up the lane toward the road.

Dan jerked his head toward the house then. "Inside," he said. "The three of you."

In single file they went up the steps and into the house. Dan marched them into the bedroom and pulled the door shut behind them, with the final caution: "Stay there a while. If you come out before I've gone, I'll plug you sure."

They wouldn't stay in there long, but they'd stay long enough for him to get out of sight in the brush.

At a silent run, he circled the house and swung up on Rusty. He rode the horse out of the yard at a careful walk, but as soon as he was out of earshot of the house, his spurs urged the sorrel into a gallop. In a few moments the house, the yard, and the unconscious Mallory were lost to his view.

Well, at least he hadn't killed anybody. They wanted him for rustling, and now for resisting arrest. But there was no murder warrant out for him — at least not yet.

Chapter Six

With no idea at the moment of where he was going, all that mattered to Dan Iles was to put as many miles as possible between himself and Sheriff Tate. He tried to decide what the men he had eluded would expect him to do. A trail led up through the rimrock directly opposite the ranch. In all probability they would expect him to use that. It was the fastest route to Utah.

How long did he have? An hour? Two? Hell, he had a lot more than that. Likely he had a full four hours before they could even start. They'd first have to catch horses, but instead of trying to repair their saddles they probably would hitch those two horses to the buckboard, and drive to Sundance after more horses. They would need more men, also, and provisions for what might turn into a long chase. Starting from Sundance, maybe they could cut his trail before dark. But maybe they wouldn't. He could hope they couldn't.

Instead of taking the rimrock trail, Dan

climbed until he was right at the foot of the rim. Then paralleling the rim, he rode south. Crumbling rock at the foot of the rim would hide his trail, would cause Tate and Mallory further confusion tomorrow when they finally found it.

Ever since Mallory and the sheriff had ridden into the yard this afternoon, Dan had been going on nerve alone. Now his hands shook. Weakness came over him like a shock. He clung to the saddle horn and let the horse pick its own way along.

Where was he going? What would he do? He had no answers to these questions. An overpowering sense of hopelessness began to overwhelm him.

One of the guns fell out of his belt and clattered on the rocks. He dismounted, retrieved it. He sorted through the four, found one to his liking, an almost new .45, buried the other three weapons under some rocks, and stuffed the .45 back in his belt.

In early dusk, Dan dismounted at a spot where water seeped out of the rocks. He built a fire from dead aspen branches that had fallen from the rim, and set his coffee pot under the slow trickle of water that dripped down off the rocks. He heated a can of beans in the skillet, made coffee.

He intended to travel all night. He was

afraid to show a fire in the dark, yet he knew he ought to have something hot in his stomach. At dusk, however, neither smoke nor flame was visible from any great distance, but as soon as his coffee had boiled, Dan stamped out the fire.

He hunkered down with his back against the rocks and forced himself to eat slowly. Forcing himself to rest afterward was somewhat harder, but he lay down and closed his eyes. Every nerve in his body seemed to be tightly strung, and his ears were tuned to the distance, waiting for that telltale fall of a single rock, the snap of a branch.

Even though he knew pursuers could not possibly have caught up with him yet, he could not control these impulses within himself. Once he got used to being hunted, he would find sleep easy to achieve, in half-hour snatches, whenever opportunity presented itself. He might become accustomed, in a way, to getting along with such snatches of sleep, but he would never cease longing for a full, uninterrupted eight hours, untroubled by anxiety or fear.

Dusk was a deep, soft gray when he mounted again. He dropped downward, across the slide, into the ancient fastnesses of the cedars. At the bottom, he crossed a creek, climbed again, and took the first trail that led up through the rim to the top of the plateau.

From here, he could look over the valley he had just crossed, could see the mesa top where the sheriff and his posse would be seeking him. The night hours lagged and slowly slipped away. But at last Dan began to experience an odd sort of pleasure from it all, began to appreciate the excitement of it.

In truth, although he did not put the thought into words, there was extreme excitement in being hunted, second only to the excitement of being the hunter. It was an excitement that tarnished quickly, but it was well that he felt it now, for it made him forget his fear, made his brain begin to work.

In the first chill gray of dawn, he cut a trail that led left toward the rim again, and took this without hesitation. He waited until he was in the cedars before he built his fire. He had no water for coffee, so simply heated beans and ate them quickly. Again, he carefully stamped out the embers of his fire.

He was tired now, desperately so. Reason told him he could chance a few hours' sleep, but he was thirsty, so he continued on downward until he struck the creek in the valley. There he drank and washed.

Squatted, with his face and hands wet, he

heard a twig snap behind him. Instinct told him to whirl, to grab for his gun. But a new sense of caution was rapidly developing in him. Apparently ignoring the sound, he finished washing and stood up, wiping water from his eyes with his sleeve.

He dropped his hands and wiped the palms of them once on his pants. Then, with all the speed he could muster, he snaked the .44 out of its holster and whirled.

A voice said softly: "Slow, but not too bad for a kid." It was a voice that was strange to Dan Iles, one he had never heard before.

Dan never finished centering the muzzle of his gun on the man. With his thumb curled over the hammer, with the weapon uncocked, he stopped and let the gun drop until it hung at arm's length at his side.

The voice said: "You think fast, too."

Dan felt a rising resentment. "What do you want?"

The stranger stepped from behind a light screen of willows. He was a slender, red-bearded, red-faced man. His eyes were an odd, pale blue. He held his gun almost negligently, but its muzzle carefully followed Dan's every move. He said, his voice soft, almost gentle: "Why son, I thought maybe you might have some coffee or beans or something."

Dan was still suspicious, but he slipped his gun back into its holster. He had no choice. But as the stranger did the same immediately, Dan couldn't help thinking: *Now I've got an even break if I want to try again.* But he knew this wasn't true. The stranger made him feel awfully young, awfully helpless — even foolish. He grumbled: "I got beans and coffee both. I guess some meat would taste kind of good."

"That's the way to talk." The man stooped and began to gather dry sticks. Dan helped him. When both had an armload, the stranger began to shave a stick with a pocketknife. Hunkered down, watching the flames mount, he murmured: "Coffee. Hell, it's been a long time. Hurry up, kid."

Dan got the coffee and pot from his saddle. He filled the pot at the creek, and the red-bearded stranger arranged it over the flames. When the water boiled, Dan threw in a handful of coffee. The stranger got a hindquarter of venison and a cup from his own saddle. Dan got down a couple cans of beans, his last.

The stranger put the beans in the frying pan and stirred them with a stick as they heated. Dan studied him. While appearing to be indolent and relaxed, he was alert enough as could be seen by watching him closely. Not a bird moved in the trees overhead that his eyes didn't see. Dan's every gesture came under his indolent scrutiny. There was wildness in him, wildness like that of an animal. And Dan had a feeling that he was dangerous, a very dangerous man.

There was something else about him, too, that Dan could sense but could not name. And it was this, not his wildness, that gave birth to the uneasiness Dan felt in his presence. It was almost the same uneasiness that could be felt when near a diamondback — a combination of fear, respect, and repugnance.

Since Dan had eaten beans up in the cedars, he left these beans to the stranger, who wolfed down both cans as though he had not eaten for a week. Dan ate fried venison. But both drank coffee, almost half a pot apiece.

Afterward the stranger hunkered against a rock and rolled a cigarette. When he finished, he passed the makings to Dan.

Dan never smoked much. But like all boys, he had practiced rolling cigarettes until he was fairly proficient. It was one of the skills of men that boys learned avidly whether they liked smoking or not. Dan found the smoke comforting this morning. He caught the stranger peering at him oddly and looked away, disturbed.

The stranger said: "I'm Red Velton, boy."

"Dan Iles."

Velton seemed to expect Dan to recognize his name, but Dan did not. Velton said: "Kind of queer to see a kid your age on the dodge."

"How you know I'm on the dodge?"

Velton chuckled mirthlessly. "It's written on a man's face and in his actions. A kid that ain't running don't go for his gun when he hears a noise behind him. A man gets a hunted look about him, Dan, that's easy enough spotted."

Dan was silent.

After a while, Velton asked: "You kill somebody, Dan?"

Dan shook his head. "Not yet." His mouth was a thin line, his eyes hard.

"But you mean to, huh?"

"I sure do."

Dan had a feeling that spilling confidences to this man was unwise, but he couldn't help himself. Velton had a sympathetic manner that encouraged confidences. And however much Dan had matured in the last couple of weeks, he was still a boy, with a boy's uncertainties and lack of confidence. Velton was older, near the age Dan's father had been.

So Dan talked. He told Velton the whole

story in clipped, angry sentences.

When he had finished, Velton whistled slowly. "Boy! They gave it to you good, didn't they?" He frowned, thoughtful for a few moments. Finally he asked: "This Mallory. You reckon he's after your place?"

Dan shrugged. "Don't know why he should be. He's got a big enough place of his own. If he had more water. . . ."

"Maybe that's it! Water!"

"I hadn't thought of that."

"With you gone, there ain't no one to claim your water, is there? They can't sell your place, so it just sits there idle. Mallory gets the use of it and your water, too. After so many years of that, the water ain't yours no more. It's Mallory's by the right of appropriation."

Dan frowned. Velton's reasoning could explain a lot of things. Those falsely branded calves. Mallory's apparently causeless persecution of him.

Velton appeared to have forgotten Dan's trouble. And the beans had made him drowsy. He stared at Dan for a long time thoughtfully, until Dan began to feel uneasy. At last the red-bearded man said: "I need some sleep. You reckon you can stay awake and watch a while?"

"I ought to be moving along."

Velton shook his head. "Don't play yourself out. Let the posse do that." He gestured with a thumb at the top of the mesa. "They're up there. You're down here. If they took time to comb out every little draw, they'd never get anywhere. They figure you're scared. They know you're a kid. They won't even give you credit for sense enough to hole up somewheres. They'll figure you to run till your horse drops."

Dan thought about that. It made sense, he had to admit. His own inclination was to run continually, ceaselessly, as fast as his horse would carry him. Inside, he could feel himself relaxing. He nodded. "All right, I'll stay awake. Go on and get your sleep."

Velton stared at him for a moment more, as though trying to read his mind, his character, his intentions. Velton had probably been running all his life. Running, a man likely found little trust in his fellow man. Plainly Velton was trying to decide whether it was safe for him to sleep, leaving Dan to watch. He must have decided it was, for he finally lay back, his hands clasped behind his head.

The fire began to smoke, and Dan put it out with water he carried from the creek. He scrubbed out his skillet and coffee pot with sand, and packed them back on his saddle.

His horse was grazing, but was hampered by the bit, so Dan slipped it out of his mouth, leaving on the bridle.

After a while, Velton's eyes closed and his breathing turned slow and regular. Dan studied the man covertly. And he began to wonder if this was the way he must himself live now. The idea was repulsive to him. Yet there seemed to be no solution other than that. If he traveled to some other part of the country, then he had to forget the ILS and let Mallory have it.

The very thought angered him. No! He wouldn't do that. Herb Iles had spent a lifetime building the ILS. Dan's mother had borne him there, and had died there doing it. All of the material things that spelled familiarity and security for him were at the ILS. And there was Dan's conviction of rightness, his resentment at Mallory's persecution of him. No, he'd not run now, for if he did, he would spend his life running.

He sat down and watched the rippling motion of the creek. A fish jumped in a sun-lighted pool. A big one.

Grinning for the first time in days, Dan unwound fishing line and hook from the crown of his hat. He cut a willow wand with his pocketknife. With the same knife, he dug in the moist ground until he found an anemic-looking worm with which he baited the hook.

Holding the makeshift rod before him, he wriggled through the grass until his face looked down upon the pool. He dropped in his baited hook, watched it float downward into the dark and secret depths of the pool.

A shadow moved, far down there. Moved with a lightning swirl. Dan felt a savage tug on his line. The willow bent almost double. Dan kept a strain on the pole, and let the fish fight. Frantically, back and forth, up and down, the fish went.

For half an hour, Dan forgot his trouble, forgot Mallory and Red Velton, forgot where he was. He fought the fish and in the end he won, holding the fish's exhausted head above water while he reached down and hooked a finger in its gill.

The fish must have weighed a full three pounds. Dan broke its neck and cleaned it on the bank of the stream. He wrapped it in wet grass and packed it in leaves.

Then he came out of a fisherman's world of unreality and became a man again, a worried, thoroughly frightened one. He could see no end to his troubles. He was a wanted rustler, and there was no way on earth of proving his innocence. Gloom and awful depression settled over him, and he dropped his head wearily into his hands.

Chapter Seven

It was late afternoon before Velton awoke. Dan was drowsy, terribly so. He stared at Velton with blank and weary eyes. Velton got up, looked at Dan, and said: "You're played out, too. Take a nap. I'll call you for supper."

"There's a fish under that pile of leaves over there."

Velton crossed over and unwrapped the fish. He held it up by its gill admiringly. "Lordy, boy, I'm glad I ran into you." He whistled. "Trout! Real cutthroat trout!" He rewrapped the fish tenderly, reverently.

When Dan lay down, he felt an odd security, an odd sense of well-being. He was asleep almost instantly. But his sleep was not peaceful. He dreamed of Susan Mallory, felt her body hot and tight against him, felt the stirrings of manhood in himself. He felt the brutal smash of Mallory's fists, and whimpered a little in his sleep. He saw his father's body, still and limp in the dust, and strained and heaved as he loaded it atop the horse. And he refought the battle with

Mallory and the sheriff, and fled into the afternoon and through the night.

It was dusk when he awoke. For a moment he lay still, hearing the sizzling noise the trout made in the frying pan. Smoke drifted over him from the fire, and it was this, perhaps, that had awakened him.

He got up and stumbled to the creek. He doused his face and head in the icy water, then went over to the fire and spread his hands before it. Velton took the frying pan off the fire and, with a sheath knife, cut the fish in two.

Dan wolfed his down in a few short minutes. He drank two cups of coffee, then Velton doused the fire, leaving them in utter darkness. Silently they ate, each thinking his own secret thoughts. At length, Velton got up and fumbled through the darkness until he found his saddle. Dan could hear him settling down, rolling himself in his blankets.

Dan walked out and checked the picket rope on the horses. He found his own saddle and untied his small blanket roll. He lay down, pillowing his head on the saddle.

He rubbed his face with a hand, feeling the bristly fuzz growing there. He thought: *Need a shave.* But he had no razor, and likely Velton had none, either. Well, it didn't matter. He drowsed. But now, with his utter exhaustion eased by the afternoon nap, he did not sleep soundly. He woke at frequent intervals and lay listening. This was the way, he realized, that a hunted man lived. Never knowing really sound sleep, never relaxing his alertness.

Just before dawn, he heard Velton get up. At first, he paid no particular attention, but just lay watching soundlessly. But Velton did not walk off a few yards from camp and then come back. He went out to where the horses were. Dan could hear the stir he made, catching them. Dan's horse and Velton's, too.

Velton left his horse fifty yards from camp and returned quietly for his saddle. He took pains to muffle the low clink of cinch buckle and bridle bit. Dan thought, outraged: *Why the damned son-of-a-bitch is stealing my horse!* He sighed, and rolled, as though in sleep. Velton froze, watching him. Dan made his breathing slow and regular. Velton turned his back.

Carefully Dan eased the .44 out of its holster. He lifted it and centered by feel on Velton's back. Thumb on hammer, he said: "Now freeze, damn you, or I'll blow your guts out!"

At the same instant, he let the hammer

come back, its click killed by the sound of his voice. Although Velton was only a shadow, Dan could sense the tautness that instantly stilled the man. Velton held his saddle in his left hand. His right was free, but he had to turn. And he would be slowed by the saddle, unless he dropped it, which would give him away.

For what seemed to be an eternity, Velton stood just that way. Dan carefully pulled his feet under him and stood up. His gun never wavered for an instant. Velton was beat, for the moment. But Dan knew the man's ears were tuned to each small sound. If he thought he had the slightest chance, he'd whirl and draw.

Dan didn't mean to give him that chance. And he intended to draw the diamond-back's fangs. He approached, walking slowly, carefully.

Velton said: "Kid, I only wanted to see if you had the stuff. I been looking for someone to travel with, but I couldn't load myself down with a kid unless he was tough, could I?"

"I don't want to travel with you."

"Why not? Gun slinging is an art, kid. Some take to it pretty natural, but you still got to learn it. There's a lot of things I can teach you."

"Like how to catch horse thieves?"

Velton laughed nervously. "No. You don't need much teaching in that, looks like. Trouble with kids is a man's likely to underestimate them." His voice was rueful. "I won't do that again with you, Dan."

Dan was just behind him now. Swiftly his hand snaked out and yanked Velton's gun. He stepped back, back a full fifteen feet. Far enough so that Velton couldn't rush him, too far for him to throw a saddle.

Dan said: "You can turn around now."

Velton did. He said: "Now what, Dan? You going to hold a gun on me forever?"

Dan didn't know the answer to that. He felt just a little foolish. But he was angered, too. Angered by the man's perfidy. Angered by injustice. He'd had his fill of that back at the ILS from Mallory and the sheriff. Now he was finding it here in Velton.

He was disillusioned, bitter. Had his father been the only decent man in the world? Were all men this way, stealing, cheating, lying? Were all women like Susan Mallory, not knowing the meaning of honor, of decency? Dan didn't know. He hated to believe they were. But what else was there to believe?

Well, Dan guessed, he could play the hand the way the cards fell. But he was beginning to realize that to do that he had to be able to meet all comers on equal terms. He had to know the gun. Here was a man who claimed he could teach him. And Velton had asked him a question. Now he repeated it. "You going to hold a gun on me forever, Dan?"

Dan's voice did not sound like his own. It said: "I might kill you. Ain't that what generally happens to horse thieves?"

"What would it gain you, kid?" Velton's voice was plainly nervous.

"A horse and saddle. A couple of guns. Killing you would gain me that much. And I'd be rid of you. I could quit watching my back."

Velton laughed. "But you won't do it." Apparently he had sensed some drawing back in Dan, some innate reluctance to take a life.

Dan grunted: "No, I won't now." Dawn had lightened the sky as they talked. The landscape was a cold, cheerless gray. But a man could see a little now. Dan said: "How do I know you won't kill me when I return your gun?"

"You don't know. But I won't, kid. A man gets lonesome. I figured you for a punk that'd slow me down. I can see I was wrong. You string along with me, kid, and I'll show you the ropes."

Dan thought about that. He hadn't much choice, really. There were but three ways out of this. Kill Velton. Steal his horse and leave him afoot. Or give him back his gun. The first two alternatives were offensive to Dan. And the third was risky. But what the hell? What did he have to live for? He tossed Velton's gun across to him, and Velton caught it by the muzzle, holstering it immediately.

Dan held his own gun for a moment, then shoved it back into his holster. He said: "All right. You're fast. You can beat me, if you want to try. And if you figure on killing me or stealing my horse, you'd just as well go ahead now."

Velton's beard made his expression secret. His eyes glittered. For a while Dan thought he was going to try, but at last the red-haired man grunted — "Dan, you'll do." — and, turning, began to gather wood for the morning fire.

The days passed. Dan, not caring now what happened to him, relaxed fully. He slept well. His body grew hard and lean. His nerves became like iron.

Velton had a dog-eared pack of cards, and they played poker on a blanket. Dan spent hours drawing, from every conceivable position. Velton taught him to sling his holster low on his thigh, and rigged him a tie-down so that it would not bind when he drew. He carved the holster down so that the gun's trigger guard was fully exposed. He soaped the holster on the inside, and filed off the front sight. These were small things, but he taught Dan their importance. Small oversights were paid for in lives. He wanted to see that Dan was guilty of none.

Dan had a natural aptitude for the gun. His reflexes were like lightning. After two weeks of unending practice, Velton admitted ruefully that Dan could beat him to the draw, any time, from any position. "I never seen nothing like it," he said. "You're a natural." His face turned grave. "But there's more to it than drawing. It don't make a hell of a lot of difference in a fight which man gets his iron out first. Not who gets off the first shot. It's the man who makes the first hit that wins. So you got to learn to get that first hit."

It meant ammunition, and they didn't have too much. Dan practiced sparingly with what they did have. He and Red Velton would stand side by side, would draw at a signal, would fire at a bean can on the ground twenty-five feet away. He learned to take his time, to hit the bean can with his first shot. And one day he realized that he no longer feared Velton. That was the day he saddled up and said to Velton: "I'm leaving. You coming along?"

Velton nodded. He looked at Dan, and could not repress a shiver. He said: "I shouldn't go with you."

Dan's eyebrows lifted. "Why not?"

Velton made a mirthless grin behind his beard. His devious mind was, for once, honest. He said: "Because sooner or later, you're going to kill me. Because I hate you and you despise me. I should have killed you when I could, and taken your horse."

"Why didn't you?"

Velton shrugged. "Because I'm a fool, I guess. Maybe being kind of proud had something to do with it. I got a glimpse of what could be made out of you. I couldn't keep from making it."

Although it puzzled him, Dan shrugged that off. Velton caught his horse and saddled up. Together they rode south.

Chapter Eight

Mallory and Tate rode for three days without picking up Dan Iles's trail. On the morning of the fourth day, Mallory said: "Sheriff, let's give it up. I've got work to do . . . spring branding, irrigating, all kinds of things. I want to take a trip over to Denver and see Susan. Let the damned kid go. We don't know he stole more'n them two calves, and I got 'em back. I'll vent the ILS brand and put my own on 'em."

Tate was relieved. Dan Iles had surprised him. He hadn't thought an eighteen-year-old would be clever enough to get away. He'd thought it was a matter of a couple of days' riding. But it had turned into more than that.

In a way, Tate was glad Dan had got away. True, his pride smarted because of the licking Dan had given him in his office that night. It smarted worse because of the horse Dan had killed for him, because of the gun Dan had taken from him. He'd have been rough on Dan if he could have caught him right away. But time mellowed anger, sometimes killing resentment altogether.

Tate was not a small man, or a man without feelings. He admitted that Susan Mallory was probably a slut. He'd suspected that for a long time. A man hears things in the saloons, if he just sits quiet and listens.

Dan hadn't had much chance against Susan, with her experience, her charm, and her utter lack of principle. So Tate couldn't bring himself to blame Dan much for his affair with Susan. Also, the sheriff was leaning more and more to the belief that Herb Iles *had* been murdered, shot from ambush, just as Dan had claimed. During the chase, he'd studied Mallory and had found something wrong. Nothing he could put a finger on, of course. Just a feeling. But a law man doesn't make arrests on feelings. Officially, Iles had been killed in self-defense. Tate knew he'd never prove otherwise, not with Susan and Mallory sticking so closely together in their stories.

On the seventh day, Tate and Mallory rode into Sundance. Tate pulled in before his office. Mallory made no move to dismount.

"I'll go right home," he said.

Tate tugged at his mustache, studying Mallory. He could feel less liking for the man today than ever before. Mallory's eyebrows pulled together at his scrutiny. "What's the matter, Tate?"

Mallory was big, big and ruthless. In his eyes was no softness at all. His jaw was long and hard, covered now with a week's growth of gray bristles. His mouth was a thin, colorless line.

Tate said: "I was thinking. I expect I ought to send out Wanted notices on Dan. Sooner or later, he'll hit some town. Then he'll be picked up and brought back."

Tate was honestly reluctant to send out notices on Dan. But he knew he had to. It was his job. Unless Mallory refused to press charges, and that was unlikely.

Mallory surprised him. "Don't do that, Tate. Let the kid go. I got my calves back. If any more turn up, I'll get them, too. There ain't no use hounding the kid."

Tate's eyes widened briefly. He saw no compassion in Mallory, no pity for Dan. And he was vastly puzzled. He said: "Mallory, that's big of you. You mean you want to drop the charges against Dan in Sundance, too?"

"I didn't say that, Sheriff. I didn't say that at all. I said there wasn't no use hounding the kid, and there ain't. But I don't want him coming back here. He accuses me of murdering his pa. And he's been. . . ." — Mallory flushed, looked pained, but went on determinedly — "well, friendly with Susan. You can see why I wouldn't want him around. So long as he stays on your Wanted list in Sundance, he ain't likely to come back."

Tate dismounted. He knew he ought to feel relieved, because this had turned out just the way he wanted it to. But he didn't feel relieved — only uneasy and vaguely troubled. He watched Mallory ride away, remembering the slate-gray color of Mallory's eyes. Like the sky on a cold, blustery winter day. Like snow, drifted and dirtied, in the deep gray of dusk. Chill and without feeling.

Well, Dan was gone, was safely away. If he stayed away from Sundance, out of Tate's county, he'd not be troubled. But would he stay away? Considering this, Tate was able at last to put a finger on the vague uneasiness that was so troubling to him. No, Dan wouldn't stay away. And when he came back, there'd be hell to pay, with Tate right smack in the middle of it.

Red Velton, riding ahead, reined up at the crest of a low rise of ground and stared downward in silence. Dan Iles moved up beside him.

This was the extreme western edge of Colorado, a land of bare ground, of stunted sage and greasewood, of weird, eroded rock formations. Below lay a ranch, the first they had encountered since leaving their camp.

Dan could see tiny figures moving around down there. A corral, three sides built of poles, the fourth formed by a sheer rock wall, was filled to bursting with cattle. A fire was going near the corral gate, and, as Dan watched, a rider came out of the press of cattle in the corral, dragging a calf on the end of his rope.

The scared bleat of the calf drifted up to him on the still air. A man's shout. And a woman's voice.

He looked at Velton. "You hear that?"

"Damned right." Velton was grinning in an odd way. "Damned right I heard that. A woman. A young one, too, from the sound of it."

There was a strange timbre in Velton's voice, an intent glassiness about his eyes. His beard hid the expression on his face, if there was any.

Dan asked: "What'll we do? Ride in? Maybe they'd give us a job."

"Sure . . . sure. Let's ride in." Velton licked his lips.

He gigged his horse with his heels, and the

animal moved downward off the rise. Dan followed, painfully conscious of his appearance. He was incredibly dirty. He was unshaven. His skin was blackened by the sun until he looked like an Indian. Except for that black stubble of fuzz on his cheeks and chin. He rubbed it ruefully.

He was afraid the two of them would look pretty rough to that outfit down there, with their guns tied down and the look of outlawry upon them both. But Velton was riding in confidently enough, his eyes shifting back and forth avidly, seeking, searching.

Two men were working the corral with horses and ropes. A little knot of freshly branded calves huddled outside the corral, over near the face of rock in a corner. Their mothers grouped nearby inside the corral, and a continual bawling passed back and forth between the two groups, with the calves trying to get their heads through the poles to nurse.

Two more men worked the fire, catching and throwing the calves as they were dragged in, tying them expertly, then going to work with hot iron and knife. A fifth man sat on a wooden box in the sun, watching. One of his legs was stretched out before him, and a crutch leaned against him. He was probably in his sixties, but it was obvious that he was in charge.

The sixth person was the girl whose voice they had heard, and she didn't look like a girl, until one was close to her, until the swell of her breasts beneath her man's tight shirt was seen, and the fullness of her hips encased in Levi's. Suddenly Dan and Velton caught her attention, and she whispered something to the old man. He looked up, replied to her, and she crossed over the corral. When she returned, she carried a Winchester carbine.

The old man's eyes were frosty, without welcome.

Velton smiled ingratiatingly, never taking his eyes from the girl. "Howdy," he said. "Saw your place as we was going by. Taking on any hands?"

The old man started to speak, but the girl cut in: "Not your kind. Move along."

She lifted the rifle until it centered steadily on Velton. She seemed to ignore Dan, and he found this disconcerting. He took his glance from the man and studied the girl. Her face was too thin, he decided, for real beauty. Her hair, a deep, rich brown, was brushed straight back and tied with a ribbon. The ribbon was her only concession to femininity. Otherwise, she was dressed like a man. Her eyes were brown, her lips full, her mouth wide. High cheekbones and faintly hollow cheeks deprived her of prettiness but, oddly, added to her attraction for Dan. When she moved, it was quickly, nervously. She repeated in a flat, unfriendly voice: "Move along, I said."

Dan shrugged, flushing slightly. "Well, all right, if you feel that way about it. Come on, Red."

"Wait a minute." Velton's voice was oily. He kept staring at the girl. "That ain't no way to treat a couple of strangers. It's kind of the custom to ask a man to light and eat. If you ain't got jobs, you ain't got jobs, but it ain't going to hurt you to feed a couple of hungry riders once in a while."

Dan said impatiently: "Come on, Red." He started to ride away.

The old man spoke for the first time. "That wouldn't hurt none, Noreen. Let 'em fill their bellies. Then they can go."

She was reluctant, but she did not attempt to argue. "All right." She turned to Dan and Red. Red's steady glance upon her brought a light flush of anger to her cheeks. She said: "Get down. Wash water and soap's over at the pump." She gestured toward the house, a low, log structure with a roof that barely escaped being flat.

Dan smiled. "Thanks, miss."

He tied his horse to the corral out of the way, and walked stiffly toward the house. He drank first. The water was brackish and full of alkali. Then, while Velton worked the pump, he soaked his head and neck and lathered recklessly. He rinsed off the lather and groped for the square of toweling that hung near the pump. Velton handed it to him. Rubbing his fuzzy stubble, Dan again wished for a razor. He'd buy one the first time they hit a town.

As he worked the pump handle for Velton, he said: "That girl'd be pretty if she'd wear a dress."

Velton only grunted. He seemed to have lost interest in the girl entirely, which was surprising after the avid interest he had shown in her up to now.

They lolled in the shade, smoking, until the branding crew knocked off for dinner. The girl came to the house, and they could hear her clattering around in the kitchen.

After a while, Noreen came to the door and shouted: "Come and get it!"

Dan went in last, following Velton. He found himself a place at the long table. There was a big bowl of chicken and dumplings in the middle of the table. There were

250

fresh-baked bread and lots of fresh butter and jam. Boiled potatoes. A couple of kinds of canned vegetables. Dan was ashamed of the way he ate. But he couldn't seem to help himself.

The crew ignored him, ignored Velton. The old man was nowhere to be seen. As soon as they were finished, the crew got up and left.

Dan stopped on his way out, saying a little shyly: "Miss, that was a meal like you dream about. You reckon there's something I could do to kind of make up for the way I hogged it?"

Her smile transformed her face, made her eyes sparkle, gave a softer curve to her lips. Dan could see her beauty when she smiled, for all the somberness left her face, all the sternness went out of her eyes. The smile quickly went away as she saw Velton, lingering behind him at the door. Her eyes were harsh again. "No. Just go. Get your horses and ride."

Dan nodded. "All right. Good bye."

He went outside, cursing Velton under his breath. Velton followed him to the corral. Dan mounted and waited. When Velton was up, he reined south again.

They traveled all the afternoon. At four, they came to a watered draw where a few scattered cottonwoods grew. Velton called immediately from behind: "Let's camp here. We ain't in no awful hurry. If we keep on, we might have to dry camp."

Dan dismounted, off saddled, and staked out his horse. Velton did the same. Then they gathered wood for the fire. Their rations were slim now. Venison that Velton had jerked while they were camped for so long. A little tea. No more than that.

Dan was not yet hungry, so he lay back against the trunk of a cottonwood and shaped a smoke.

Velton said: "Hell, I was hoping they'd give us a job back there. But they're all through branding. That was the last bunch. I heard one of those hands say they were pulling out this afternoon."

"I wouldn't mind a job there myself. Chicken and dumplings! I wonder how long it'll be before I taste anything like that again."

After a little while their conversation died, as it always did. Dan could talk to Velton when there was something specific to talk about, but he knew a growing dislike for the man and a mounting distrust. He did not enjoy Velton's company.

Silence dragged, and at last, near sundown, Red got up, stretching. He walked over to his horse, threw his saddle up, and led the animal back to camp. He said: "Saw deer sign this afternoon. Sundown's a good time to hunt. See you later."

Dan nodded. He watched Red ride out, go up a long rise, and drop into a draw. Dan still watched, wondering why he did. He saw a buck deer come running back out of the draw, saw him pause on the crest of the ridge. He waited for Velton's shot, but it didn't come. The deer disappeared, and Dan didn't see Red again.

The sun went down. Orange and mauve and ochre touched the rims of the mesas, changing slowly to violet, and finally to gray. Velton didn't return, and Dan did not hear him shoot.

He got up suddenly and caught his horse. Saddled, he followed the course Velton had taken upon leaving camp. It was rapidly darkening. But before complete darkness dropped over the land, Dan reached the spot where Velton had spooked out the deer. The deer's tracks passed within fifty yards of where Velton had halted to watch him. Velton had not dismounted, not fired. He had lied about going hunting. He had lied.

Dan touched his horse with his spurs. At a lope, he went along Red Velton's plain trail. It continued south, but gradually it began to tend westerly. And finally it was going north. In the last fading light, Dan came to where Velton's trail had passed the draw where the two were camped.

Velton had still been heading north. Toward the ranch where they had nooned — toward that girl called Noreen, unprotected tonight except for a crippled old man. Rage flamed suddenly in Dan Iles, and he urged Rusty on anxiously with his spurs, cursing himself because he had been blind and a fool.

Chapter Nine

The branding crew ate at six, and by seven they were gone, riding north in a group. Noreen Delaney's father, old Vince, was again dozing in the parlor on the horsehair sofa. Noreen was tired. She stared dispiritedly at the mess in the kitchen for a few moments. Shrugging, then, she went outside and sat down on the sagging porch step.

She felt gritty, dirty. She was tired of wearing men's clothes. But she was glad the branding was done for another spring. She was glad the crew was gone. Spring roundup, spring branding was always hard. Particularly since Noreen not only handled feeding the crew, but also came out between meals and helped at the branding fire.

She stared despondently at the bare landscape, deeply bronzed by the setting sun. She remembered the two men who had ridden in at noon, looking for food, looking for jobs. She thought of the red-whiskered man, and a shiver ran down her spine. There was a bad one. The way he'd looked at her had actually made her flesh crawl.

She forced her thoughts away from him and remembered the young one. He had seemed different. How did he happen to be traveling with the other who looked like an outlaw? Noreen smiled at her own thoughts. Because he had been young and good to look upon, she was giving him credit for being different. But he carried the same stamp the older man did, wore the same low-slung gun, had a wild, dangerous look.

The air was warm for spring. It felt soft and pleasant against her face. With both hands, she rubbed her forehead. She thought: *Gosh, it would be good to wear a dress again.* She sat there for a few moments, her thoughts idle. Why not? Why not walk down to the creek a quarter mile away? There was a deep pool down there in which she often bathed and swam when there were no men working on the ranch. She knew she'd feel better for a bath and clean, fresh clothes. And Vince would still be sleeping in the parlor when she returned.

She got up, but when she went into the kitchen, she stared at the stacks of dirty dishes with dismay, shaking her head. No use to get cleaned up, then have to come back to this. She'd have to do this first.

She lighted a lamp, and pitched in vigorously. Outside the moon rose, and climbed across the sky. Vince still slept in the parlor, soundly now, snoring loudly. Noreen smiled.

She finished cleaning up the day's dishes. For a moment she hesitated about the bath at the creek, weighing the comfort of that against the more immediate comfort of bed and sleep. In the end, she tiptoed through the house to her bedroom. She got fresh underclothes and a dress, a clean towel, and soap. She tiptoed out again without waking Vince and, hurrying now, headed for the pool in the creek.

Usually in spring, the air grew cool as soon as the sun went down. But this was late spring, and tonight was different. Warm air still hung over the land, unstirred by even a small breeze. At the creek, Noreen took off her clothes and splashed into the pool. Even the water was warm, having been heated all day by the sun. Noreen found it pleasant, relaxing.

She soaped herself leisurely, then ducked down to rinse. She was beginning to feel better already. The tiredness seemed to go out of her body, and she began to sing softly. But it was getting late. If Vince should wake, he would worry when he found her gone. Regretfully she stepped out onto the bank and began to dry herself. The towel was rough, and it stirred and stimulated her circulation.

Suddenly, frighteningly so, the air seemed to cool. Or Noreen did. She could feel cold shivers running up and down her spine. Or were they shivers of fear? Oddly uneasy, she took a step toward her clothes. She was being silly, she told herself. There was nothing to fear here, nothing to cause uneasiness. Then she heard it — a snapping twig, followed by a crashing of brush, as though some heavy animal, frightened, were running. The sounds were coming close. Noreen poised like a frightened doe, uncertain, terrified.

Then, in the moonlight, fifteen feet away, she saw him. She saw his bushy beard, his eyes glittering. She heard the hoarse animal sounds that issued from his mouth. She had stopped to snatch for her clothes to cover herself, when she knew instantly she had made a mistake. She should have run. Without doubt she could have escaped, but now it was too late! The instant she had spent reaching for her clothes had ruined all chance of escape.

She knew the man now. It was the red-bearded man who had watched her so avidly all during the noon meal, the one who had made her so uneasy, so uncomfortable. He'd come back!

She leaped aside, tried to dodge him, but felt his hands close on her arm. She jerked away, but his fingers were like talons, biting into her flesh. Panic flooded over her in a tide. She opened her mouth and screamed. Then she was down, sprawled on the ground, and the man with the red beard was struggling with her.

She had never heard the sound that Red Velton heard — the running pound of horse's hoofs. But as suddenly as he had seized her, he released her. Noreen snatched at her clothes again, instinctively covering herself with them. Velton was crouched ten feet away, facing the sound of the approaching hoofs.

Noreen was seized with an uncontrollable shuddering. Her teeth chattered, as though from cold. Low, whimpering sounds of fear came from her lips, and she could not stop them.

A voice, wild with fury, came out of the moon-dappled darkness. "Red! Damn you . . . !"

The young man's voice. Now she would have two of them to fight!

But the man called Red shouted back, his voice tight, crazed with frustration: "I should have killed you, when I had the chance. But I'll kill you now. I'll kill you now!"

★ ★ ★

Just over a quarter mile from the ranch, Dan Iles had heard the girl's scream. It had come from the creek, off to his right. Instantly he had reined that way, never slacking his speed.

The moon was bright, and a moment later he saw the two figures through a break in the trees, struggling on the ground. Almost at once the figures separated, and Velton stood crouched, facing him.

The girl was white in the moonlight. She snatched up her clothes and held them before her. Her pitiful whimpering kindled a fury in Dan that surpassed anything he had ever known. He heard his own voice cursing Red, and he heard Red's words: "I'll kill you now!"

Maybe. Maybe not. Dan swung off the running horse fifty feet from Velton. Moonlight made the scene like day. Velton's hand hung stiff and tense at his side.

Dan had no thought for anything but his rage, no eyes for anything save Velton. Yet some warning voice within himself seemed to say: *Cool off, or he* will *kill you.*

A slow step at a time, he moved toward Velton. This was not shooting at bean cans. This was a test. Fear cooled Dan's rage momentarily. He couldn't let Velton kill him.

He couldn't! Not that he was afraid to die. But dying would leave this girl, Noreen, at Velton's mercy.

Dan's left arm swung with his walking motion, but his right did not. Its distance from the gun grips never varied. It was like a claw, and Dan's mind was saying, over and over: *It ain't the one who gets off the first shot that wins. It's the one who gets the first hit.* And Velton's words: *Sooner or later, you're going to kill me. Because I hate you and you despise me.*

The girl's whimpering was like an accompaniment to this endless walk, and fear built up in Dan Iles until he could scarcely control his impulse to whirl, to run. Yet his measured stride never varied. Neither did his cold glance waver.

He was twenty feet from Velton, when the man moved. Velton's hand snaked down, came up with his gun. Incredibly fast. Dan had no remembrance of starting for his own gun. But he must have. He could feel the grips, smooth against his palm, could feel the hammer under his thumb. His mind kept saying: *Take your time.* But there was no time. Only split seconds until eternity. His mind registered surprise that all fear was gone. *Take your time. Take your time. It's the first hit that counts, not the first shot.*

The gun bucked back against his palm.

Velton took a hasty backward step, as though struck by some monstrous force. His gun, not quite level, blasted brightly orange in the moonlight. His bullet buried itself harmlessly at Dan's feet. The gun dropped from his hand. Clutching his shirt front, he staggered a couple of steps toward Dan. Then he folded quietly.

Dan's first reaction was shock. Velton was dead. Dan himself had killed him. Then he heard Noreen's whimpering. She was staring at him in utter terror. He took a step toward her, halted at her sudden cry. He said: "I'll go catch the horses. Then I'll take you back to the house."

He caught his own horse, then Velton's. He tied Velton's animal to a tree and walked back to the creek, leading Rusty.

All fear of him was not gone from Noreen. She was fully dressed, holding her extra clothing in her arms. She didn't speak, nor did Dan. In silence they walked back toward the house.

Dan was embarrassed. He had seen her the way no man should see a woman until they are married. And he was disturbed. He had killed a man. It was a sensation similar to the one he had felt at twelve when he had killed his first deer. One instant there was life, movement, feelings, fear. The next there was nothing. Nothing but a limp, cooling body on the ground.

Dan was amazed at himself as well. He had beaten Red Velton to the draw. Even taking his time, making sure of the first hit, he had still beaten the man. This realization brought a new thought to his mind: *I'm ready now. I'm ready to go back for Mallory.*

Chapter Ten

Lamps were lit in the house. Vince Delaney was standing at the kitchen door, his crutch supporting him, the Winchester in his hands. When he saw the white of Noreen's dress, something drained out of him, and he sagged against the doorjamb.

Coming closer, Dan could see that the old man's face was lined and gray with worry. Noreen called in a voice that had no strength: "It's all right, Dad. It's all right now."

Vince Delaney moved aside, and Noreen went into the kitchen. Dan halted at the door, saying: "Well, I've got things to do. I'll take care of Red, and then I'll be going."

Noreen returned to the door. "You will not! You come right in here and sit down. I want to thank you, and Dad will want to thank you, too, when he knows what you did."

Dan went in meekly. He sat down at the kitchen table. Noreen stirred up the fire and put on the coffee pot. "Have you had supper?"

"No, but. . . ."

"But nothing. I'll fix you some."

She was firm and brisk, but there was a lot of softness in her eyes when she looked at him. She looked entirely different in a dress, Dan thought. Feminine. Pretty. No, not pretty exactly. Like a columbine in an aspen grove. Delicate. Fragile.

Vince Delaney leaned his rifle against the wall and came over and sat down. "When is someone going to get around to telling me what happened?"

Noreen told him. About her bath at the creek. About Red Velton. Her face whitened with her remembered fear. Involuntarily she shuddered.

Delaney said: "And this boy killed him?" He was unbelieving.

Noreen seemed proud. Her cheeks flushed with pride. But Dan had a knot of something forming in his stomach. Maybe he looked funny, because Delaney put out a gnarled hand and touched his arm.

"First time, eh, boy?"

Dan nodded. Noreen poured him a cup of coffee. He sipped it, but nausea was gathering in his stomach. His hands began to shake, and he had to put the cup down. He said: "He taught me how to use a gun. He knew I'd kill him someday, but he taught me, anyway. That's funny, isn't it?"

"No. Ironic, maybe. Not funny. Death is never funny, son."

Dan wondered why Delaney reminded him of his own father. There was nothing about either Delaney's appearance or manner that even remotely resembled Herb Iles's. Maybe it was Dan's need that made him see a similarity.

Delaney asked: "How'd you get mixed up with a man like that Velton anyway, son?"

Dan told him. Prodded by Delaney's gentle questions, he told the whole story — about Susan Mallory, John Mallory, about the beating he had taken from John, about Herb Iles's murder, about the sheriff and his refusal to arrest Mallory. He told about the calves he had been accused of stealing, about the fight with the sheriff's posse, and his subsequent flight.

When he had finished, for some reason he felt better. Noreen put a plate of steaming chicken and dumplings left over from dinner before him, and he began to eat. He realized that he was famished, and that his nausea was gone. The way Noreen was looking at him made Dan feel weak, made all his newly found manhood threaten to leave him. He kept his eyes on the plate and ate swiftly.

Delaney said: "You know where you've

been. Do you know where you're going?"

"You bet I do. I'm going back to Sundance now. I'm going to kill Mallory." He tried to keep bravado out of his voice.

"And after that?"

Dan shrugged. "I don't know."

Noreen sat down beside him and now broke into the conversation. Her tone was indignant. "I'll tell you. After that, you're on the dodge with a murder warrant out for you. The first time you hit a town, the sheriff will try to arrest you. He won't have a chance, Dan, because you'll have to kill him. And you *will* kill him. You're that good. I saw you tonight. You're a. . . ." She stopped.

Dan asked: "I'm a what?"

"It's frightening. You're a natural born gunman. I never saw anything that frightened me quite as much as watching you tonight. That gun you carry isn't wood and steel. It's part of your body. You use it that naturally. And your eyes, Dan. You ought to have seen what they looked like tonight."

Dan got up quickly. He said formally, stiffly: "I'm sorry I scared you. I'll be going now."

He started for the door, but Noreen rushed around and put herself in front of him. With a hand on each side of the doorjamb she stopped him.

She said: "You didn't let me finish. After you kill that first unfortunate sheriff, who tries to arrest you, you'll run again. Maybe with a posse on your trail. You'll be lucky, if they get you. Because if they don't, you'll kill again. And again, and again. There's only one thing that will stop you, and that's being killed yourself. You can never quit, and there'll come a time when you want to quit."

"How do you know all this? How can you be so sure?"

"Because I had a brother." There were tears now, standing out unashamedly in her eyes. "I had a brother." She looked across his shoulders at old Vince Delaney. She said: "Did you ever hear of Kid Delaney?"

Dan nodded. He had heard of Kid Delaney. Everyone had. But Kid Delaney was dead now, had been for a couple of years or more. Kid Delaney had died with about seven slugs in him. But he had killed two men and wounded three in his last fight, the fight that had become one of the West's legends.

Dan was hesitating. Noreen was no more than seventeen herself. But what she did then proved her a woman grown. She stepped close to Dan, took his hands, and put his arms around her. Her own arms stole around his neck. She pulled his head down and kissed him, and she let her body mold itself warmly and excitingly against him.

Dan's arms tightened. He returned her kiss. And then Noreen stepped away. She said softly: "Stay with us a while, Dan. Stay with us until you've had time to think. Don't make up your mind tonight."

She won, as, of course, she had known she would. She had used her womanhood the way Dan used his gun, skillfully and with a purpose.

Dan went outside and unsaddled Rusty, and turned him loose to graze. He carried a shovel down to the creek and dug a grave for Velton, taking only Velton's gun and belt off of him before he rolled him in. He rode Velton's horse back to the house and turned him loose, too. Then, dead tired, he stumbled to the bunkhouse and fell, fully dressed, upon one of the bunks.

Dan Iles stayed at Delaney's VD Bar. The days turned into weeks, the weeks into months. He still wore his gun, but he wore it differently now — higher on his waist, with no tie-down. He wore it the way ordinary 'punchers wore theirs, and this way it offered no particular challenge to other gunmen. It put no brand upon Dan Iles, no brand that could be read from a quarter mile away.

In August he drove Noreen to Moab in the buckboard, and there she caught the stage for Denver. She told him she had an aunt whom she always visited in late summer before the fall work commenced. Dan believed her. He had no reason not to.

There was someone in Denver whom Noreen wanted to see, all right. But it was not her aunt. It was Susan Mallory.

Noreen had watched Dan all through the summer. It had been obvious to her from the first that he had not forgotten Sundance. He had not forgotten Mallory, and his need for vengeance still rankled within him. He was undecided, and for the moment, at least, Noreen could hold him at the VD Bar. But for how long? Someday his need would become too strong for him, and then he would leave, would head back to Sundance.

She knew that she need not worry about Dan as long as she was gone. She had his promise to stay, and, besides, Vince was a virtual cripple of late, scarcely able to get around. Dan would feel an obligation to stay and look after Vince. So Noreen turned her thoughts toward Denver. Susan Mallory was the key to this puzzle, for Susan Mallory had lied. Now, she must be made to tell the truth.

The stage crawled east, gnawing at the endless miles. The country changed from the sage and mesa country to pine and peak country. Snow still lay on some of the higher crests. On the fourth day they crossed the Divide and began the descent to the plain, flat and endless in the distance.

Noreen was tired, near exhaustion from the endless pounding she had received as the stage thundered over rough and rocky roads. Yet in spite of her weariness, excitement stirred in her as the stage rolled into Denver's dusty streets.

Never had she seen anything like this. Buggies and carriages moved in stately procession along the streets. Men were in fine broadcloth and beaver hats. Women were in silks and brocades. Brick buildings towered three full stories into the sky.

Noreen got used to the wonders of the city quickly. She wandered from hotel to hotel, inquiring, but she did not find Susan Mallory. She had no picture to help her, only Dan's description, and that would fit dozens of women. When the hotels were exhausted, Noreen tried the rooming houses. Again she failed to find Susan Mallory.

Finally, with all other means exhausted, she inserted an advertisement in the *News*. She had been in Denver over a week.

That evening she had a visitor. She knew immediately as she opened her door that this was Susan. She said, smiling coolly: "Won't you come in?"

Susan was obviously suspicious. It was apparent to Noreen that only curiosity and fear had prompted Susan to answer the ad. Susan was dressed in a beautiful brocade gown decorated with rhinestones. She wore a white fur wrap. She asked, her eyes hard: "What do you want? Who are you?"

"I'm Noreen Delaney." All of Noreen's confidence suddenly departed. How could she get the truth from this self-possessed woman? She said: "Do you remember Dan Iles?"

Susan started, and her eyes widened briefly. "Yes. What about him?"

"He intends to try and kill your husband. He knows that your husband killed his father from ambush and falsely accused him of rustling. He has tried to get satisfaction from the law, but. . . ." She shrugged.

Susan asked coldly: "What is your connection with him? What is your interest in this?"

Noreen hesitated. She said simply: "I love

him. I don't want to see him hounded and chased all over the West until he is killed, which is what would happen if he goes back and kills your husband."

"What do you want from me?"

"The truth."

"I'd have to go back to Sundance. I'd have to admit that I lied before."

"You'll do it?" Noreen was trembling, weak.

The woman was silent for several moments. "I won't go back, no . . . but because it will also serve a purpose of my own, I'll give you a written statement. Will that do?"

Noreen didn't know. She thought it might, but she didn't know. It was apparent, however, that a statement was all she was going to get right now. She nodded. "It will have to do."

Susan sat down at the table. Noreen brought a sheet of paper and pen, and Susan began to write. When she had finished, she went to the door and called to someone down the hall. A man came into the room immediately, and Susan asked him to witness her statement.

He was an oldish man, expensively dressed. Susan said: "This is Mister Lindhorst."

Noreen nodded to him and smiled. She

thought she was beginning to understand. Susan and Lindhorst went to the door.

Susan said: "I hope this will be sufficient. If it isn't, I guess I'll have to go back to Sundance."

"Thank you. I hope that won't be necessary."

Noreen closed the door on them and leaned against it, smiling shakily. She understood Susan Mallory's ready cooperation now, all right. Susan wanted to marry Lindhorst, who was quite obviously wealthy. But she could not so long as she remained married to Mallory who, insanely jealous and possessive, would not give her a divorce. This, then, was Susan Mallory's way of ridding herself of her husband. If he were convicted of murder he would be executed. Then Susan would be free to marry Lindhorst.

Noreen was suddenly glad she had not told Susan of the change in Dan Iles. Susan had not believed Dan capable of killing Mallory or she would never have given Noreen this statement.

The way seemed clear to Noreen now, and hastily she began to pack. She could not wait to tell Dan her news.

Chapter Eleven

Since Noreen arrived at Moab without having previously notified Dan at the VD Bar, there was, of course, no one to meet her. She hired a buckboard and a team of horses and set out for home alone.

After six hours of steady driving, she pulled into the yard at the VD Bar. Dan came running out of the house, and Noreen, laughing and crying at once, handed him the statement Susan Mallory had signed.

He read it through and then, incredulously, read it again. He was going back! He was going back!

All the summer's tenseness and bitterness seemed to drain out of him. He helped Noreen down, lifted her bags from the rear of the buckboard. As he stuffed the paper into his pocket, his eyes glowed with his thoughts of home, of freedom.

Noreen felt a sudden emptiness. She watched him lead the buckboard team across the yard. Listlessly she lifted her bags and carried them into the house.

She began to realize then what she had done. Perhaps two hundred miles lay between Sundance and the VD Bar. But it might as well be a thousand. When Dan left here, she'd never see him again. He had his father's ranch at Sundance to care for. She had old Vince Delaney here. She had the VD Bar to think about. She was an incident in Dan Iles's life, one he would soon forget. Hopelessly she stared at Vince, who sat puffing his pipe in the big leather-covered chair in the parlor.

She said: "I did what I wanted to do. I got the truth from Susan Mallory." Her voice turned bitter. "But now he'll go away. He'll forget me." Tears stood in her eyes. "Dad, why are women such fools?"

Vince moved his crippled leg painfully. He said: "You couldn't have kept him here forever, honey. The thing's been eating at him all summer. He told me while you were gone that he'd be leaving right after fall roundup. He was going back, honey."

Noreen sank into a chair. Suddenly the strain of the six-hour drive from Moab and of the endless stage journey from Denver made their demands on her strength. Perhaps she might have broken down, might have wept out of her frustration and disappointment, had she not heard Dan in the kitchen. She dabbed at her eyes and stood up.

He came in, holding his hat in his hands. He seemed older today. Older and quieter. He said: "I don't guess I can ever thank you enough for what you've done. I guess I'll always remember."

Noreen felt like screaming at him: *Do you think I can ever forget? You fool! You fool! Are you stone blind?* But she didn't do that. She smiled a tight little smile and gave him her hand. "We've got things to be thankful to you for, too, Dan. Good luck."

Vince cleared his throat, but Noreen said: "No, Dad. Let him go."

Only when he was gone did Noreen run to her room and throw herself down on the bed. She wept until it seemed she could weep no more. Then she slept, completely and utterly exhausted and no longer caring about anything.

Dan rode steadily all that night. At daybreak he camped, picketed Rusty out, and ate some biscuits and cold, cooked bacon that Noreen had put into his grub sack. He lay down and slept for a couple of hours, then he was up and riding again.

He knew he should be elated, relaxed, completely happy. He was going home. He was going back to the house at the ILS, to the old, familiar things he had known all of his life. He was going back to his memories of his father. He was going back to clear his name. He was not going back with his gun in his hand, but the right way, seeking only justice. And he knew justice would not be denied him this time. Then why did heaviness and depression ride his thoughts? He shrugged.

All day he kept riding, but that night he camped and slept the night away. And at dusk of the third day, he came into Sundance.

He knew he should go directly to Sheriff Tate's office. But, somehow, he wanted to spend tonight at the ILS. He wanted to see the familiar things again. So he skirted the town in the deepening dusk and took the road that led upcountry to the ILS and the Ox-Yoke.

What would he find? Half a year had passed since he had last seen the place. Half a year, and things changed in that time. He would find the fields dry for lack of irrigation, the hay stunted and poor. He would find weeds waist-high around the ranch house. He would find the corrals deserted and dry.

Then he caught himself thinking not of home, but of Noreen Delaney. He caught himself remembering her face, the expression in her eyes. He remembered vividly the night he had killed Velton, the night she had thrown herself into his arms and asked him to stay.

He forced his thoughts to concentrate on the ILS, on John Mallory, who tomorrow would be lodged in jail to wait for his trial and his hanging. This was the important thing — vengeance for the killing of his father, the clearing of his name, the carrying on of the ranch his father had built.

The night advanced, and Rusty plodded on. At ten, Dan turned in at the gate and started down the lane. It was a dark night, starless, moonless. A haze of cloud lay across the sky. Dan could not see over ten feet ahead of him. But he knew the lay of the land, knew where each fence line was, each building. He kept his eyes fixed on the spot where the house would appear out of darkness.

But it did not appear. There was only emptiness, bare ground where the ranch house should be. Dan swung down. He tripped over something — a charred timber. He banged up against the rock fireplace that rose like a blackened specter into the sky. The house was gone, burned to the ground! Dan stood stunned in the charred ruins for a long moment.

Frantically, then, he ran across the yard. This was something he had to know. Had the house at the ILS burned by accident, or by Mallory's design? He would soon find out. At the barn he stumbled and fell again, fell into charred ruins and ashes. The chicken house had also been burned, and the bunkhouse was gone. There was nothing left. Nothing!

Was this what he had waited all summer for, what he had ridden the last three days toward? He felt in his pocket for Susan Mallory's statement. Rage kindled in him, and it was almost as though he had never gone away. He totaled up in his mind all for which Mallory had to answer. The beating, the killing of Herb Iles, the false evidence of rustling that had put Dan on the run. And now this.

It was not enough that the Ox-Yoke rancher had hounded Dan out of the country so that he could steal the ILS water. He'd had to burn everything that was dear to Dan, every remembered thing!

For an eternity Dan stood, silent and still, in the utter dark. He could hear Rusty moving around, could hear the faint squeak of saddle leather. Everything in him demanded that he ignore this paper in his pocket, that he ride now to the Ox-Yoke and call Mallory out of his house.

Something stopped him. He did not know exactly what it was. Perhaps it was the paper in his pocket that Noreen had gone to so much trouble to get. Perhaps it was the memory of Noreen herself. Or maybe it was that Dan remembered the emotions that had tugged at him as he yanked out his gun and fired at Velton. Perhaps he could recall the sensation of loss he had felt, seeing Velton, whom he hated, dead on the ground.

Dan mounted, but it was toward Sundance that he rode. He would give Tate a chance, an opportunity to do what was right. If Tate did not do it, then Dan himself would take over from there. Nothing would stop him. Nothing on earth. Before morning, he intended to see Mallory either in jail, or dead!

It was after midnight when he rode slowly into Sundance. Rusty was exhausted, near the end of his endurance. He walked wearily, head down, listlessly. Dan did not try to hurry him. He had waited a long time for this. There was no rush now.

The town was dark except for lamplight that glowed from the windows of the town's two saloons. Horses, half a dozen of them, were racked before the saloons. A quiet night in town. A quiet night, so far.

Dan realized that he was a wanted man in Sundance, that it would be dangerous for him to be seen. He rode to the deserted livery stable, off saddled Rusty, and put him into a stall. He filled the hay manger, and the horse began to eat gratefully. Dan went back into the street.

A drunken 'puncher came from one of the saloons and crawled up onto his horse. He jogged out of town, singing to himself. Dan walked along the street, and a black-and-white dog came out and yapped shrilly at his heels.

Tate's house was clear over at the edge of town. Two great maples shaded his yard, which was neatly grassed and fenced. Dan opened the picket gate and went up the walk. The house was dark, as he had expected it to be. He began to feel nervous, tight inside. He'd given Tate a bad time the last time they'd met, and the time before that. Had Tate cooled down, or had he nurtured resentment and been only waiting for a chance to line his sights on Dan?

Dan shrugged. He'd find out. He knocked on the door loudly. At first, there was only silence in the depths of the house. Then he heard a stir overhead and a voice called from an upstairs window: "What the hell you want?"

Tate's voice. Dan stepped down off the porch and out onto the lawn where he could look up at the window.

He said: "Easy does it, Sheriff. I'm not looking for trouble. It's Dan Iles."

He could hear Tate's low whistle. After that, nothing. He saw the gleam of a lamp upstairs that disappeared, then later glowed from the downstairs windows. He went up onto the porch. Tate came to the door, the lamp in one hand, a gun in the other. He was plainly nervous, but wide awake now.

Dan said: "Light on the trigger, Sheriff. I've got a statement signed by Susan Mallory that I want you to read."

Tate stood aside, and Dan went in. The sheriff took a long look at him, then put down his gun. Dan handed him the statement, and the sheriff read it, his eyes widening.

"I suspected this," he muttered, "but what the hell could I do, Dan?"

"You can do something now. He burnt me out, didn't he?"

Tate shrugged. He tried to meet Dan's eyes. He said: "I guess you've got a pretty rotten opinion of me, maybe of the law in general. But Dan, without proof, the law is helpless. Can't you see that?"

Dan said: "You've got proof now."

"You don't want to wait until morning?" Dan didn't answer, and Tate stared at him for a long time. Finally he shook his head. "No. You don't want to wait. We'll go get him tonight."

A woman in a long nightgown and flannel wrapper came down the stairs, alarm in her face. "What's the matter?"

Tate crossed to her. "Go back to bed. I'm going after John Mallory."

He finished dressing, got his coat, and came back to Dan. "What about those calves, Dan?"

Dan shrugged. "He could have run an ILS brand on 'em himself. He always wanted our water, and that'd be a good way to get it. Run me out of the country and help himself."

"You got a horse?"

"No. Mine's played out."

"I've got an extra one. Come on."

Dan followed him through the house and out the back door. Things were falling into place the way they ought to. Tate was an honest sheriff and full of co-operation now. There were two of them to get Mallory, and they'd take him by surprise. Things were perfect.

Dan wondered why he had to keep telling himself these things. He wondered why uneasiness and doubt stayed so insistently right on the edge of his thoughts. He wondered why he couldn't believe that it was going to be as easy as it appeared to be. And he wondered why his hand kept straying instinctively to the grips of his gun, as though he sought to reassure himself.

Chapter Twelve

For three hours, Noreen slept. When she awoke, it was a few moments before her consciousness picked up all that had happened and arranged events in orderly sequence. Instantly, then, her deep sense of depression, of hopelessness, returned.

She got up, brushed her hair, and went out into the parlor. Vince still sat where she had left him. If only he were not so helpless! If only she could leave, could follow Dan. Pride told her that women do not run after their men. But pride was no good at a time like this. Pride was a weak substitute for the strength of a man's arms.

Vince stared at her thoughtfully for a long time. At last he said: "You want him, don't you?"

Noreen started to protest, an instinctive reflex. But her protest died unspoken. She was too honest with herself to lie; she was too honest with Vince, and always had been. She said helplessly: "I guess I do. But what am I going to do about it?"

"Follow him."

"I can't leave you alone."

"I can get along. I get around all right."

Noreen wanted to. Oh God, she wanted to!

Vince said: "You can be back in a week. I'll get along fine for that long."

She sank down beside him. "Oh, Dad, do you think . . . ?"

"You won't get him staying here. He's got a ranch at Sundance. He'll stay to straighten it out. A man forgets faster'n a woman does, honey. Saddle up and go."

Her pride stirred again. If he could forget so fast . . . ? But she made herself face facts. Did she want to live out her life with the shreds of pride, or with Dan? She said: "All right, I'll do it."

She spent the afternoon carrying in wood, baking bread, cooking things for Vince that would keep. And at dusk she rode out, clad as she had been when Dan first had seen her, in Levi's and shirt, with boots and spurs and a bright bandanna over her head. Behind her saddle were tied blankets and enough food for the trip. She was doing something, and that was the important thing.

To Dan, the two-hour ride to the Ox-Yoke

was the longest he had ever taken in all his life. Tate rode silently, a tired man, an aging one. Dan rode behind him.

The clouds overhead thinned and drifted away, and the stars winked brightly, casting their negligible glow on the land below. That odd feeling of unease persisted in Dan, and he tried to pin it down, tried to rationalize the reason for it. What would Mallory do when confronted by Tate and Dan Iles, when told about Susan's statement? What could he do?

The answer to that was fairly simple. All Dan had to do was to ask himself what he would do in like circumstances. And he knew. No matter what the odds, no matter what the circumstances, Mallory would fight. He would fight the way he'd fought Dan's father that day last spring. He would fight to win, and the devil take the hindmost. He would fight treacherously, from ambush if need be. He would throw what 'punchers he had into the fight, for he would know that his own survival depended not only on Dan's death but on the sheriff's as well.

Dan wondered if Tate's thoughts were as somber as his own. From Tate's slumped posture in his saddle, he guessed they were.

They went past the ILS gate, and anger

again began to rise in Dan. He said, speaking ahead to Tate: "How you going to work this, Sheriff? You know he ain't going to give up, don't you?"

Tate turned in his saddle as he spoke. "I guess I do. But you take on a certain responsibility when you pin on a law man's star. You kind of agree to a lot of things without nothing ever being said about them. You agree to give a wanted man a chance before you shoot. You agree not to let your gun be judge and jury and executioner, no matter what the circumstances or the odds."

He was silent for a quarter mile, and then he said: "I reckon it'll have to be that way tonight. I want Mallory alive, if I can get him that way. That means he gets the first shot at me, if he wants it."

"And after that?"

"Why, after that I reckon we'll play the cards the way they fall."

Tate rode in silence then until they reached the Ox-Yoke big gate. Reining in, he said: "Dan, you'll play it my way or you'll stay here. Which is it going to be?"

Dan hesitated. He wanted Mallory, wanted to kill him. Yet he knew how much Noreen had gone through to prevent just this. He recognized in himself a reluctance that accounted for his going to Tate tonight instead of directly to Mallory. Also, in the past two hours he had acquired more respect for the law, more respect for Tate as its representative, than he'd ever known before. So he said: "You're running the show. I'll play along with you until one of us is hit. After that, I'll play it my own way."

"Fair enough. Come on."

They went through the gate and rode slowly and carefully down the long lane. From the corral, a horse nickered, and before Tate could clamp a hand over his horse's nostrils, the animal answered.

Tate dismounted before the house and tramped stolidly up onto the porch. He hammered on the door with his fist, shouting: "Mallory! It's Tate. Open up. I want to talk to you."

Dan stood behind Sheriff Tate, a little to one side. The house remained dark, but he could hear movement inside. Fear clawed at him. He was recalling the feel of Mallory's enormous, solid fists, the utter madness in the man's eyes, their complete coldness. He heard the door swing open, but in the darkness could see nothing.

Tate spoke, saying: "Mallory, you're under arrest. I've got a statement from your wife admitting she lied about Herb Iles's death. Light a lamp and come quietly, John."

"Who's that with you?" Mallory's voice teetered on the edge of madness. It was low, tight, barely under control.

Tate said: "Never mind . . . never mind. Just come along."

To Dan, this was foolhardiness. Mallory, standing in the doorway, was completely invisible in the darkness. Yet Tate, silhouetted faintly against the slight starlight in the yard, made a good target.

Behind them, a lamp glowed suddenly in the bunkhouse. In a moment more they would have men behind them to reckon with. Dan's thoughts kept crying at Tate. *For God's sake, don't just stand there! Do something! Draw your gun. Shoot! Or jump inside. But do something!*

The bunkhouse door opened and slammed back against the bunkhouse wall. A hasty glance showed Dan two men as they came out and started toward the house.

One of them yelled: "Hey! What's going on?"

It gave Dan an eerie feeling, knowing that Mallory stood there in the doorway, but not being able to see him. An unpleasant chill ran along his spine. Then it came, as Dan had known it had to come — a tongue of flame leaping toward Tate out of the doorway. Tate grunted as though slammed in the stomach by a ponderous fist. The shock of the bullet turned him half around. And Dan suddenly realized that Tate did not even have his gun out.

Foolishness. Bravery. Tate had demonstrated both of these. And now it was too late for him to get out his gun. He staggered sideward across the porch, making a scuffling sound on the plank floor.

Dan's hand had gone automatically for his gun the instant Mallory had fired. Now it was coming up, hammer back. It bucked, and his shot went into the floor, but Mallory had jumped aside.

Mallory's voice roared inside the house: "Boys! Get the coyote! He's on the porch!"

Instantly the guns of the two 'punchers began their staccato barking. Bullets thumped into the walls of the house beside Dan. There was little choice here. He could see that. Inside Mallory waited for his dim figure to appear at the door. Outside, Mallory's 'punchers raked the porch with their fire. Tate was a slumped and silent shape over on the far end of the porch.

The sheriff's voice came, twisted with pain but plain enough: "Go get him, boy. He's yours now. "

As though this had been what he was waiting for, Dan drove his body forward and went through the door in a shallow dive. Almost beside him, Mallory's gun flared, momentarily blinding him. He hit the floor inside, rolling, still clutching his gun. He banged against a chair and knocked it over. Immediately Mallory's gun roared again, deafening in this confined space.

Dan, off balance and still rolling, nevertheless snapped a shot at the flare, just hoping. It was a forlorn hope, and his hit was not serious. Yet it drew a bellow of rage from Mallory, and moved him back against the far wall.

Silently, cat-like, Dan pulled his feet under him and got up. He backed across the room, circling, trying to get Mallory's figure against the dim light filtering through door and window. He called: "You're all done, Mallory! But don't give up. Don't do that. Keep right on fighting until I kill you."

He stepped aside as Mallory triggered three fast bullets toward him. He laughed, tauntingly. "Gun empty, Mallory?" He had heard the click of the loading gate on Mallory's gun, the rasp of the ejector, and the light plunk of empties on the floor.

He kept circling, still trying to see his antagonist. He felt a chair against his leg. He lifted it silently and, with a savage heave, threw it across the room. Mallory blasted at it twice, and Dan saw the faint outline of his body behind the flares. It was enough. His gun muzzle moved imperceptibly, with no conscious prompting, and acrid smoke whirled across the room before him. The bullet, striking Mallory, made a solid smacking sound that was nearly inaudible, so closely did it blend with the roar of Dan's gun.

Obscenity bubbled from Mallory's lips, but he did not go down.

Dan asked coldly: "Enough, Mallory? Throw your gun across the room."

Mallory's voice was dull, filled with pain. "All right. Don't shoot any more."

Something heavy hit the floor and skidded across it. Outside, Tate was calling to the men in the yard. "Quit shooting, boys! This is sheriff's business. Mallory's wanted for murder. Quit shooting, boys, or I'll take you in with him."

Maybe Tate didn't fully convince them, but their guns fell silent. Tate's voice went on, growing weaker. "Go back to the bunk-house and wait. Go on . . . go on!" Impatience edged into his voice.

Dan was crossing the floor toward Mallory. He said: "Face to the wall, Mallory. I'm coming across."

He wished he could see. With his left hand he fumbled in his shirt pocket and got a match. He thumbed it alight awkwardly, And then he knew he had been duped. Mallory had thrown something on the floor, but he had not thrown his gun. His left hand was across his belly, and he was bent slightly forward. In the glow from the match he seemed enormous, a hulking, huge figure filled with incalculable menace. His gun wavered, then centered on Dan.

Dan was caught almost entirely by surprise. His gun was lowered, its muzzle pointing at the floor. There was no time for thought, but there was time for his belly to grow cold, to tighten against the expected impact of Mallory's bullet.

His gun was coming up, but it was too slow. The match burned Dan's fingers, and he did not even notice it or let go. Then, with a shocking impact, Mallory's bullet slammed into his left shoulder.

Its force was terrible. Dan, helpless, was turned away from Mallory. But his gun came back, centered, and jumped. His bullet struck Mallory in the throat, silencing the shout of triumph.

The match had gone out. Dan didn't strike another. Dazed, shocked, he staggered to the door. He stepped out onto the porch, and turned toward Tate.

Tate said: "Dan?"

"Uhn-huh."

"You got him then?"

"Yeah. I gave him a chance to live, Sheriff. But he didn't want it."

Dan saw a horse standing at the porch steps. Over where the sheriff was there were two figures. Two of them.

Tate said: "Dan, you've got a visitor."

She came running across the porch, but she stopped as she reached him. He dropped his gun into holster. He knew he must be delirious, but he could have sworn that dim figure was Noreen's!

She said softly: "Dan, I've chased you two hundred miles. Leave me a little pride."

This time it was Dan who took her hands and placed them around his neck. His right arm circled her and pulled her tightly, hard against him. His lips came down and found hers.

His senses whirled, but somewhere he could hear Tate's deep chuckling voice: "Dan, you've got to ride the open trails from here on out."

When Dan could talk, he said softly: "Sheriff, it'll be a pleasure."

COVENTRY LIBRARIES

Please return this book on or before
the last date stamped below.

PS130553 DISK 4

To renew any items:

Coventry City Council

- visit any Coventry Library

- go online to www.coventry.gov.uk/libraries

- telephone 024 7683 1999